"A guy has ... woman like ..."

Quinn's lips brushed Constance's ear as he said this, and he pulled her against him. She was suddenly very aware of his gender—excitedly, dangerously aware.

"A guy has to wonder what?"

"If that deep feeling goes into the bedroom with you, too," he breathed, each word tickling her ear provocatively.

This was the last stand for her feminine resistance. Deftly she ducked sideways, freeing herself from his embrace.

"In the bedroom?" she repeated, her tone bantering. "Of course it does."

"I'll bet with that clear conscience of yours, you sleep like a baby."

She stared at him for a long moment. He met her gaze and held it. Quietly she answered, "I used to."

Dear Reader,

The 20th anniversary excitement continues as we bring you a 2-in-1 collection containing brand-new novellas by two of your favorite authors: Maggie Shayne and Marilyn Pappano. *Who Do You Love?* It's an interesting question—made more complicated for these heroes and heroines because they're not quite what they seem, making the path to happily-ever-after an especially twisty one. Enjoy!

A YEAR OF LOVING DANGEROUSLY continues with *Her Secret Weapon* by bestselling writer Beverly Barton. This is a great secret-baby story—with a forgotten night of passion thrown in to make things even more exciting. Our in-line 36 HOURS spin-off continues with *A Thanksgiving To Remember*, by Margaret Watson. Suspenseful and sensual, this story shows off her talents to their fullest. Applaud the return of Justine Davis with *The Return of Luke McGuire*. There's something irresistible about a bad boy turned hero, and Justine's compelling and emotional handling of the theme will win your heart. In *The Lawman Meets His Bride*, Meagan McKinney brings her MATCHED IN MONTANA miniseries over from Desire with an exciting romance featuring a to-die-for hero. Finally, pick up *The Virgin Beauty* by Claire King and discover why this relative newcomer already has people talking about her talent.

Share the excitement—and come back next month for more!

Leslie J. Wainger
Executive Senior Editor

Please address questions and book requests to:
Silhouette Reader Service
U.S.: 3010 Walden Ave., P.O. Box 1325, Buffalo, NY 14269
Canadian: P.O. Box 609, Fort Erie, Ont. L2A 5X3

THE LAWMAN
MEETS HIS BRIDE
MEAGAN McKINNEY

Silhouette®
INTIMATE™MOMENTS®
Published by Silhouette Books
America's Publisher of Contemporary Romance

SILHOUETTE BOOKS

ISBN 0-373-27107-7

THE LAWMAN MEETS HIS BRIDE

Visit Silhouette at www.eHarlequin.com

Printed in U.S.A.

MEAGAN McKINNEY

is the author of over a dozen novels of hardcover and paperback historical and contemporary women's fiction. In addition to romance, she likes to inject mystery and thriller elements into her work. Currently she lives in the Garden District of New Orleans with her two young sons, two very self-entitled cats and a crazy red mutt. Her favorite hobbies are traveling to the Arctic and, of course, reading!

IT'S OUR 20th ANNIVERSARY!
We'll be celebrating all year,
Continuing with these fabulous titles,
On sale in October 2000.

Desire

 #1321 The Dakota Man
Joan Hohl

 #1322 Rancher's Proposition
Anne Marie Winston

#1323 First Comes Love
Elizabeth Bevarly

 #1324 Fortune's Secret Child
Shawna Delacorte

 #1325 Marooned With a Marine
Maureen Child

 #1326 Baby: MacAllister-Made
Joan Elliott Pickart

Romance

 #1474 The Acquired Bride
Teresa Southwick

#1475 Jessie's Expecting
Kasey Michaels

#1476 Snowbound Sweetheart
Judy Christenberry

 #1477 The Nanny Proposal
Donna Clayton

#1478 Raising Baby Jane
Lilian Darcy

#1479 One Fiancée To Go, Please
Jackie Braun

Special Edition

 #1351 Bachelor's Baby Promise
Barbara McMahon

 #1352 Marrying a Delacourt
Sherryl Woods

#1353 Millionaire Takes a Bride
Pamela Toth

#1354 A Bundle of Miracles
Amy Frazier

 #1355 Hidden in a Heartbeat
Patricia McLinn

#1356 Stranger in a Small Town
Ann Roth

Intimate Moments

#1033 Who Do You Love?
Maggie Shayne/
Marilyn Pappano

 #1034 Her Secret Weapon
Beverly Barton

#1035 A Thanksgiving to Remember
Margaret Watson

#1036 The Return of Luke McGuire
Justine Davis

#1037 The Lawman Meets His Bride
Meagan McKinney

#1038 The Virgin Beauty
Claire King

Chapter 1

I'll let the machine take it, Constance Adams resolved when the telephone chirred at 5:05 p.m.

After all, the business day was over. And she had been on the go, virtually nonstop, showing homes since eleven this morning. Maybe it was the freakish winter weather, unseasonably warm and sunny, that was deceiving the tourists. For some reason, it seemed as if every upwardly mobile family east of the Mississippi was clamoring for a vacation home in Mystery, Montana.

It had been a long day of smiles and small talk, and she was tired. Ginny had already gone home, and Constance was on the verge of locking up the office when the phone rang. Nonetheless, something oddly insistent about the sound, or perhaps it was only her efficient nature, made her pick up before the answering machine could click on.

"Mystery Valley Real Estate," she answered. "This is Constance Adams speaking."

"Yes, Miss Adams, I'm sure glad I caught you."

Her first impression was confusing. The male voice sounded impatient and curiously...strained, she decided. But he went on talking before she could give it any more thought.

"My name is George Henning," the voice continued, and she recognized a trace of Northeast accent in the vowels. "I wonder if it would be possible to have a quick look at one of your listings?"

"Of course, Mr. Henning. If you'll just tell me what time is convenient for—"

"No, I mean may I have a look right now? You see, I'm quite pressed for time. I need to catch a plane later, yet this cabin has just caught my eye. I like it."

"Cabin?" Constance repeated, somewhat surprised. "You must mean the place at the end of Old Mill Road?"

"Yes, that's the one."

She hesitated, her surprise tinged by annoyance. The Mill Road cabin was her listing, all right. One of Hazel McCallum's properties. And while it was a quaint, rustic hideaway in the mountains, it hardly represented a fat commission. It was a little too remote, a little too basic, for most of her clients. Still...she hadn't exactly been swamped with offers.

"Well, Mr. Henning, it *is* rather late. I mean, it would take me some time to drive up into the mountains from here. May I ask—where are you right now?"

"In front of the cabin, actually. Saw your name on the sign. I called on my cell phone."

"Oh, I see."

A cell phone, she thought. Yes, maybe that explained the curious flattened sound to his voice. At any rate, she should have simply said no, not today. But something about his urgency compelled her to hesitate, and he allowed her no time to harden her resolve.

"I know it's late, Miss Adams, and I do apologize for the inconvenience. But I really am pressed for time. This place looks fine from outside. A quick peek at the interior, and maybe we could reach terms today?"

She frowned slightly, and a skeptical dimple appeared at one corner of her thin, expressive lips. The caller sounded intelligent and well-spoken.

Yet, the urgency in his tone puzzled her—perhaps even worried her a bit.

Inexplicably, however, she found herself giving in.

"All right, Mr. Henning. Since you're in a hurry. I'll leave right now. I should be there in about forty minutes."

The moment she hung up, however, Constance realized what a stupid thing she had just agreed to do: meet a stranger, as night came on, way up on a godforsaken slope of the Rocky Mountains.

She almost called him back to cancel. But if he was catching a plane later, she reasoned, then maybe she was tossing a sale right down a rat hole. This cabin was no hot-ticket item, she reminded herself. The woman in her was nervous, but the businesswoman in her won the brief debate.

She settled on a commonsense compromise. She quickly dialled her parents' number. At twenty-eight, she was the oldest of eight brothers and sisters, five of whom still lived at home in the summer. So there was usually no problem catching someone.

"'Lo?" answered sixteen-year-old Beth Ann's voice.

"Hi, it's just me," Constance told her kid sister. "How's the home front?"

"Thanks to Pattie it's a major suckout, that's how it is," Beth retorted, anger spiking her voice. "I'd rather just stay at school until bedtime. Least I'd be with my friends. I swear to God, Connie, if Mom 'n' Dad don't give me or her your old room, I am going to move into the basement. I am so sick of her spazoid mouth."

"Look, don't drag me into your feud. You two are a circus act. Is Mom home?"

"Uh-huh. She's upstairs hanging curtains with Aunt Janet. Want me to get her?"

"Don't bother," Constance said.

In the background she heard an angry glissando of piano notes from the music room. Thirteen-year-old Pattie practicing—and no doubt in a pettish mood about it, if Constance remembered her own violin lessons accurately.

"Listen," she told her sister. "I'm on my way to show someone that cabin on Old Mill Road. It's kind of remote up there, so I'm just playing it safe. If you guys don't hear from me in, mmm, two hours or so, give me a buzz. If there's no answer at my place, try my cell phone, okay?"

"'Kay," replied Beth Ann, who seemed to resent first syllables lately.

"Hey," she added, her voice suddenly merciless in its teasing. "That's the Eighth House, 'member?"

At first Constance only wrinkled her brow in puzzlement. Then, catching on, she felt her pulse leap.

"You still remember that silliness?" she asked her sister. "I almost forgot it."

That was true, but Constance had to wonder why recalling such "silliness" made her pulse quicken. Last summer she had driven Beth Ann to Billings for a statewide cheerleading competition. Beth had talked her into visiting one of the many astrologers who set up stands in Freedom Park.

"Beware the Eighth House," the psychic had repeated several times, frowning over her chart. Meaning, Constance had assumed then, the Eighth House of the Zodiac—Death.

It was Beth Ann who first suggested that, in her case, the Eighth House also pertained to the real-estate business. She insisted that Constance check the dates of her listings. Sure enough, Hazel's cabin was indeed number eight on the list.

"Thank you for the cheery reminder," Constance said drily. "Gotta get now. You remember—if you guys don't hear from me in a couple hours, somebody call me."

"Beware," Beth Ann repeated in a ghoulish voice just before she hung up. "Beware the Eighth House!"

Only hours before he called Constance Adams, lying through his teeth, Assistant U.S. Attorney Quinn Loudon had not yet become a desperate fugitive from the very law he was sworn to uphold.

"Just take a few deep breaths and relax," Lance Pollard advised his client as the two men ascended the marble steps of the old courthouse in Kalispell, Montana. "You're a lawyer. You know the drill by now. This is just routine pretrial procedure today, I was promised. You're still a free man."

"Routine?" Quinn repeated, his smoke-colored eyes flashing anger. "All that time I was secretly assembling a case against Schrader and Whitaker, those two were laughing up their sleeves at me. They set me up, Lance. And you know damn well they killed Anders. We haven't been able to find the guy in weeks. Sheriff Cody Anders could clear me. He saw everything like I saw it. But where is he? He's dead, is what."

Quinn's jaw set in a deep knot of anger as he and his attorney moved through the magnificent hallway.

The courthouse building had been declared pompous when built at the twilight of the 19th century, but seemed impressive now at the dawn of the twenty-first. A cathedral-like vaulted ceiling topped a huge central lobby with frescoed floors.

However, the building's quaint charm eluded Quinn today. Nothing could charm him lately. Without Sheriff Anders being found, he knew he had the same chance against his accusers as an icicle in hell.

"Remember," Pollard coached him as the two men followed a stair railing of antique brass up to the private judicial chambers on the second floor. "The main focus today is the discovery process. The prosecution has to lay out whatever evidence they supposedly plan to enter against you. I'd bet some big money they haven't got diddly. You know damn good and well it's easy to get a grand-jury indictment. Barely one in five ends up in a conviction."

"Yeah, well pardon me all to hell," Quinn responded bitterly, "for not taking comfort in those odds. If I had a one in five chance of dying during an operation, would that be comforting?''

''You watch,'' Pollard insisted, as confident and relaxed as Quinn was not. ''Judge Winston will dismiss the whole mess.''

Quinn's frown etched itself deeper, emphasizing his handsome Irish upper lip.

''Mess'' didn't even begin to describe what was happening to him. A mess could be cleaned up. But this false charge against him could become a death sentence. At best it would be a permanent stain on his record and reputation. He could also be disbarred, disgraced. Worst of all, an inner demon he had hoped was dead and buried in the past might be rearing its ugly head again.

The two men approached an elderly security guard manning a metal-detection station.

''Afternoon Mr. Pollard, Mr. Loudon,'' Hank Ingman greeted them politely.

Pollard stepped through the detector's beam. Quinn handed Hank his metallic briefcase, then opened his summer-weight topcoat to show him the .38 snubby in its armpit holster.

The U.S. Attorney's office in Billings received enough threats annually to warrant arming its staff. Quinn offered the weapon, but as always the guard merely waved him around the detector.

''If their case is all smoke and mirrors like you claim,'' Quinn resumed as they bore toward Judge Winston's chambers, ''then why was my bond set so high? Christ, Lance, don't you realize Winston has the discretion to decide—today, right now—I'm a risk for flight? If he revokes my bond, the only way I'll leave this place will be in handcuffs. With Cody Anders missing and me in jail, they'll have won.''

"Quinn, you seem to think Schrader and Whitaker are little tin gods or something. One's a borderline-senile judge, the other's a paid dirt-worker for the road-construction lobby. They don't own the legal system.''

Relax, Quinn thought scornfully as anger made his jaw muscles bunch tighter. Yeah, right. Here he was, a brand-spanking-new Assistant U.S. attorney only recently sent out west from D.C. No friends in high places, no good-old-boy support network, and he had to go into hock just to pay a bail bondsman. Yet here he was, up against men so rich they drilled oil wells as tax write-offs.

Again Quinn recalled that afternoon this past April. He and Sheriff Cody Anders were standing in the quiet hallway outside Schrader's slanted-open door. Neither of them could miss the scene inside the door: Whitaker handing the thin Swiss briefcase to Schrader. *Remember, Jerry,* Whitaker's suave baritone joked, *it's not the money that matters—it's the amount.* And then both men laughing as Schrader started counting the tightly banded bills....

Pollard's voice rudely jogged Quinn back to the here and now.

"Let me do all the talking," he ordered as he knocked on the solid oak door of Winston's chambers.

Quinn took a deep breath to steady himself.

A bailiff he recognized, but didn't know by name, let both men in. Immediately, Quinn was put on guard by the ominous scene inside the comfortably appointed chambers.

As he had expected, neither Judge Jeremy Schrader nor attorney Brandon Whitaker were present. Only Judge Winston, federal internal affairs prosecutor Dolph Merriday, and two armed U.S. Marshals from the Justice Department.

The armed marshals were not routine and instantly alerted Quinn to danger. The bailiff was already armed—which most likely meant the marshals were here to "escort" Quinn to the federal lockup in Billings.

"Thank you, gentlemen, for being prompt," Judge Winston greeted the new arrivals. He bent his shaggy white, leonine head to study the notes spread out before him on a wide pecan-veneer desk. "Please have a seat."

Winston radiated a sober, proper steadiness that usually had a calming effect on Quinn. Not so today as he and Pollard slacked into chrome-and-leather chairs arranged before the desk. Suddenly aware his scalp was sweating, Quinn stood back up to remove his topcoat.

After some preliminary questions to refresh his memory, Winston addressed himself to the prosecutor.

"As you know, Dolph, one reason for this meeting is to determine what evidence you intend to proffer. But I also have to determine if said evidence warrants litigation. Now, I've read Judge Schrader's deposition. I agree it's quite damning."

Winston's stern gaze cut to Quinn, and again, despite his innocence, those old feelings of guilt lanced him deep. *The leopard cannot change its spots.*

"However," the judge continued, "at this juncture it's a classic standoff. One man's word against another's. If you have no further evidence besides hearsay, I'm inclined to dismiss right now.''

Pollard sent Quinn a triumphant grin. But Dolph Merriday spoke up quickly.

''There's more evidence, Judge Winston. Pursuant to a search warrant issued in the District of Columbia, certain items were seized during a search of Mr. Loudon's residence in Washington. *This* was discovered hidden behind a cooling vent.''

Quinn felt the blood drain from his face as Merriday unzipped a canvas tote bag and set several stacks of new one-hundred-dollar bills on Winston's desk.

''In addition to nearly seventy thousand dollars in cash,'' Merriday said, ''we found this list with it. A handwriting expert has determined that it was written by Loudon. It contains the names of various officials in the Montana Department of Highways. Loudon obviously hoped to bribe others besides Judge Schrader. It's a classic construction-kickback scheme, and Loudon hoped to be their legal go-between.''

When he first saw the money, Quinn just sat there gawking like a fool. A moment later, however, angry blood hammered at his temples. He came suddenly to his feet.

''That's a bald-faced lie!'' he shouted. ''This is a setup! They killed Cody Anders and now they aim to get rid of me. Of course I wrote the list. I intended to investigate those men. But the money was planted. Schrader and Whitaker are the perps here, not me, and Merriday is either their partner or their dupe.''

''Quinn,'' Pollard urged him, ''calm down and shut up.''

But he was past calming down, Quinn realized desperately. Already one of the U.S. marshals was reaching for the cuffs on his utility belt. A cold panic seized him—if they locked him up, he'd *never* clear his name. He would be remembered always as the very demon he had fought so hard to defeat. Either he got away now, or his fate was sealed.

In a heartbeat the .38 snubby was in his hand.

"Quinn!" Pollard shouted. "What in bleeding hell are you...?"

But it was too late for oaths, too. As the marshals went for their guns, Quinn aimed deliberately high and sent two quick slugs *thwapping* into the wall just above their heads, forcing them to take cover.

From shout to shots was a matter of mere moments. Caught completely off-guard, the bailiff had not even drawn his pistol. But he still stood, solid as a meeting house, before the room's only door. Quinn lowered one shoulder and literally knocked him aside as he bolted into the hallway.

At the end of the hall, old Hank had his gun out, his face a mask of confusion.

"Quick, Hank!" Quinn shouted as he sprinted toward him. "Judge Winston needs you!"

The guard was too rattled to question the order. Quinn barrelled past him as the two marshals and the bailiff took off after Quinn. For a moment, Hank got in their line of fire, and Quinn gained a precious lead.

Just as he hit the stairs, however, there came a hammering racket of gunfire behind him.

Quinn felt a bruising blow between his shoulder blades. But the Kevlar vest he routinely wore these days absorbed the bullet's lethal impact. He had started down the steps when a second bullet punched into the back of his left thigh.

He almost lost his footing as fiery pain erupted between his hip and his knee. But sheer determination not to let himself be sacrificed by crime barons kept him on his feet.

The wound hurt like hell, but luckily it wasn't slowing him down yet. Quinn got his second break of the day a few moments later—he heard his pursuers burst out the front of the courthouse and automatically run toward the parking structure across the street.

Earlier, however, Quinn had avoided the parking structure because of the annoying queue out front. Instead, he had parked around the side on Willow Street. That chance decision gave him a precious few minutes' head start.

It took very little time to get beyond the Kalispell city limits. Although relatively large, as Montana towns went, the population was barely 12,000. Thus he cleared town with no cops on his tail. But he knew his luck couldn't hold forever. He had to get off the roads as quickly as possible, find some place to take a better look at his wound.

With town well behind him, he unleashed the powerful V-8 engine, pushing speeds of eighty-five and ninety on the winding secondary road. Traffic remained scant as he sped toward the rugged, granite-tipped mountains. His leg felt numb and hot, but didn't seem to be bleeding much.

As the confused churning of his thoughts settled somewhat, Quinn couldn't prevent an unwelcome question from the depths of his heart. The ease with which he turned criminal back there in Kalispell, when the situation demanded: he wondered if that was just intense will to survive, or part of an inherited "skill."

His smoke-tinted eyes kept flicking to the rearview mirror. So far, still all clear. But he reminded himself he had to find a suitable place to hide, and soon. Unfortunately, he could think of absolutely no one, out West anyway, he could trust. Schrader and Whitaker knew everyone who mattered, including his own boss at the Department of Justice.

By now the engine was lugging, making the climb into the mountains. The last road sign he remembered seeing had said Old Mill Road. He knew it by name only. The car shuddered when pavement abruptly gave way to a sandy, rocky lane. There were washed-out places where the chassis scraped bottom.

Suddenly, with no warning whatsoever, Old Mill Road simply made a sharp turn and ended at a wall of trees. Just as suddenly, an old cabin loomed up on his right. Quinn had to lock the brakes and skid into the overgrown grass out front to avoid crashing into the trees.

He put the transmission in park, turned the car off, then gave the cabin a brief inspection from the car. Clearly uninhabited, judging from the overgrown yard, the split-log structure had a solid cedar-shake roof and several sash windows secured with strong batten shutters. A bright new white-and-green sign in the yard advertised MYSTERY VALLEY REAL ESTATE and listed the Realtor as Constance Adams.

Quinn, still seated in the car, saw that only a couple hours of sunlight remained. This place was well hidden. With luck, maybe he could hide here until he figured out some kind of operating plan to clear himself. Right now it was hard to even get his thoughts straight.

Breaking into the cabin, however, did not seem like

an option. That was a top-of-the-line padlock on the door, and those heavy shutters would not be easy to jimmy.

He wondered if he should just give up his wild plan—in fact, just give up, period. He was a fool to think he could elude a manhunt. For one thing, it was colder up here at this altitude—he could feel it even sitting in the car. It would be even worse after dark.

But again the harsh realization struck him with almost physical force: it wasn't just sure prison time he faced, and for a crime he never committed. It was also fatal surrender to a dark destiny, the affirmation of evil handed down in the bloodstream. At least, that's how others would see it. Quinn was no hermit who thumbed his nose at society; he cared very deeply what others thought about him.

That last thought steeled his will.

He took another look at the sign. He'd have to come up with some cock-and-bull story for the Realtor, assuming one would even come out this late. He had no clear idea how far away Mystery was. But he knew he had to try.

He took his cell phone out of his briefcase and tapped in the number on the sign.

Chapter 2

Once her Jeep started climbing out of the verdant valley, winding higher on Old Mill Road, Constance felt Beth Ann's "Eighth House" nonsense lift from her like a weight.

It was a gloriously fine day, much more like early May than late January. White tufts of cloud drifted across a sky blue as a deep lagoon. Even this late in the afternoon the sun had weight as well as warmth. It felt good through her wool skirt and blazer.

Below her, in Mystery Valley, Hazel McCallum's cattle clustered around feed stations in pastures that once again soon would be rich with sweet grass, timothy and clover. Hazel's next wheat crop would be heading up, too. If this weather held, planting season would come very early this year.

Seeing the cattle queen's realm spread out below like a panoramic painting made her decide to call Hazel. After all, this was the first nibble on that old cabin, which had been sitting vacant ever since old Ron Hupenbecker passed away back in the '80s. Hazel didn't really need the money, of course. Even the low prices for beef lately hadn't hurt her valley empire much.

But Mystery's matriarch seemed eager to know someone was living there again. "An empty house on my land," she once confided to Constance, "makes me feel like I've broken a promise."

She fished the cell phone out of her purse and tried Hazel's number.

"Hello?" Hazel answered immediately in a youthful voice that belied her seventy-five years.

"Hazel, hi, it's Connie."

"What's cookin', good-lookin'? Haven't heard from you in days. I was hoping maybe you'd run off to have a fling with one of my cowboys."

Constance laughed. "You'd love it if I did, wouldn't you?"

"So might you, so go right ahead. Tell you what…whoever you pick, I won't even dock his wages."

"Hazel, my God! I'm not even half your age, yet *I* end up doing all the blushing."

"Hon, I grew up on a ranch. Nothing makes me blush. Oh, I know you like smart men who read books and talk about great painters. A girl with your looks, going all the way overseas to spend her vacations alone at stuffy museums with idiotic names like Santa's Soap."

"It's Santa Sophia," Constance corrected her, laughing, "and it's a magnificent cathedral in Istanbul. Besides, I'm not always alone—I've met some very fascinating men at museums. Believe it or not, cowgirl, there's life outside the rodeo.''

"Oh, stuff those highbrow types. Cowboys have their good points, too.''

"Sorry, Hazel. I just can't warm up to men who treat their boots better than their women.''

Both women enjoyed a good laugh, for the joke had a nubbin of truth to it. Despite the ease and affection of their banter, however, Constance knew that Hazel was dead serious about that fling offer—and even better if it led to something more permanent.

Constance had gradually taken on the status of one of Mystery's most glaring marriage holdouts. Two of her younger siblings were married, a third engaged. When Hazel pressed her about it, she usually demurred with the excuse that she hadn't found "the one" yet. But that was only a partial truth, and Hazel knew it as well as she.

And even now the wily old cattle queen must have sensed the tenor of her thoughts.

"The burnt child fears the fire," Hazel said gently. "But, dear, does one bad burn mean you must remain in the cold forever?''

Constance slowed down for a rough section of road, trying to ignore the sudden tightness in her throat. She loved Hazel; in fact, she considered the town matriarch her closest friend. But the candid old gal sometimes forced her to confront facts Constance would rather ignore.

In the cold. Aptly put, she decided. Career-wise she was content and becoming more so. She loved her family, and she loved Mystery. Overall, she considered herself blessed and felt humble enough to admit it. But Hazel was right. Romantically speaking, she *was* trapped out in the cold—in a sort of lovers' Purgatory, that lonely and hopeless dwelling of those neither loved nor loving.

"Doug Huntington was your one permissible youthful indiscretion," Hazel assured her. "He fooled me, too, Connie, and you know very few folks ever pull the wool over this gal's eyes."

No, Connie thought, trusting was no crime. But because of trust, she had nearly married a career criminal. Only weeks before she was to marry Doug, he had suddenly left the state. But being jilted was only the beginning. About the same time he left for parts unknown, she had started receiving the first of many massive credit-card bills. Thousands of dollars in purchases she never made—and none of the cards had been stolen. He had copied the ID numbers and gone on a telephone and Internet spending spree with them.

Bad enough that she had to pay all the bills, since the cards were not reported missing. Adding final insult to grievous injury, many of the bills were for women's fine lingerie and jewelry; she had paid the bills for Doug's little sex kittens.

Her only emotional salvation from the mess was to bury it like a squirrel buries acorns. To go to the police would mean reports and maybe a trial, and she couldn't relive it again and again; it would break her. So she never reported him and never heard from him again. No one saw it outwardly in her bearing, but that trauma of the heart had orphaned all her hopes for romance. Since then, her confidence had been badly shattered when it came to judging men and their character. She doubted if she could ever pick up all the pieces again.

"Well, anyway, I didn't call you to rake up the past," she told her friend. "Possible good news. I'm on my way to show the old Hupenbecker place to a potential buyer."

"See?" Hazel perked up in triumph, never one to be sidetracked from an unpleasant topic. "You feared no one would ever call. It just needed a little time, was all. Just like you. Give it a little time, and grass will push over a stone."

"Time," Constance told her wryly, "is a rare commodity when you're trying to build up your own real-estate company."

"There's always time for love," Hazel insisted. "But you have to allow it an appointment now and then, busy lady."

"Maybe I will," Constance said with little inward conviction. "When business slows down a little. Right now it's booming, and I'm lucky if I have time to heat a microwave meal, much less meet my significant other. Speaking of business—wish me luck. Five minutes, and I'll be showing the cabin."

Before she hung up, Hazel asked, "To a man or a woman?"

"Man. One who seems used to 'politely but firmly' getting his way, too."

"Hmm," was all Hazel said to that, yet her oo-la-la tone suggested plenty. She added quickly, "Make sure to show him that lovely creek out back. Jake McCallum himself built the stone bridge over it. The State Historical Society wants to put a plaque on it, the silly featherheads. The oldest stone bridge in Montana."

"I will," Constance promised before she thumbed her phone off and put it away.

The road was almost all sand by now, and she shifted to a lower gear, the plucky little Jeep surging upward. Only now did it occur to her to wonder why a man in such a hurry would have time to be poking around out here in ''Robin Hood's barn,'' as Hazel called the wild country.

She slid through a final, dogleg bend and spotted a fairly new, loden-green Lexus parked in the overgrown clearing out front of the cabin. George Henning himself, she presumed, was leaning rather oddly against one front fender.

He looked nothing like she'd expected him to. He was no mountain man in search of an out-of-the-way cabin; instead she had a quick first impression of a business suit-clad but slightly disheveled man in his middle thirties. The short, neatly cropped black hair contrasted noticeably with his pale complexion. His handsome wingtips and subdued silk necktie suggested he belonged to the fast and furious urban jungle, not cool mountain heights.

But in spite of his dark, conservative attire, she still didn't fail to notice his pleasing physique: easily over six feet tall, wide at the shoulders, slim at the hips, an Olympic swimmer's wiry, lithe build.

That's some professional attitude, Ms. Adams, she chided herself as she parked behind his car and set the handbrake. She slid from behind the wheel, smoothing her skirt with both hands.

She felt a little flush of annoyance when he made no effort whatsoever to walk over and introduce himself. Instead, he remained leaning against his car, regally waiting for her to attend to him.

''Mr. Henning? Hello, there! I'm Constance Adams, the listing agent on the property.''

He gave her a closemouthed smile. Yet even that small politeness seemed to cause him great effort.

"Miss Adams, thanks for agreeing to come out so late. I do appreciate it."

"Please don't mention it. I enjoyed the drive, actually. I haven't been up here in some time. I tend to forget how lovely it is."

"Yes, it is," he replied curtly, a note of impatience creeping into his voice.

Instantly her annoyance at him shaded over into dislike. He was big city and too busy for her. The fact that she was putting in overtime on his account didn't rate at all. His time above all else was tantamount.

He's the customer, she tempered to herself. Still she didn't appreciate the rude treatment. Nor the strange feeling she had whenever she looked at him. It seemed horribly akin to attraction, and after Doug, she was going to have none of that.

"Since you had to wait for me," she said, "I assume you've already seen the bridge?"

He gave her a blank look. "Bridge? I…actually, no. I caught up on some work while I waited."

So he didn't even bother to explore out back. It struck her as almost incredible that anyone serious about buying the place would not have stepped around back for a peek, at least. He seemed to resent her questions and made a big production out of looking at his watch to remind her he was in a hurry.

But it wasn't her way to let others treat her like a menial servant—not even for a potential sale. *The more you pressure me, Mr. Henning, the longer it's going to take,* she resolved.

"And what kind of work do you do?" she asked

politely as the two of them began walking toward the cabin. She noticed that he favored his left leg.

"I'm self-employed," he replied, irritation clear in his tone and his face. He acted as if each word were being wrenched out of him. "I'm an investment advisor."

"How *interesting*." She was playing his game with a coy vengeance, becoming more chatty and polite in proportion as he grew irritated and terse. "And where are you from, Mr. Henning? Surely you're not from these parts, or I'd recognize you."

"Look, Miss Adams, I don't mean to rush you. Or to offend you. But I really do need to hurry. Could we just skip all the polite chitchat? My flight leaves soon."

Again the imperious tone was back, as if he were the lord of the manor and she some lowly supplicant.

Constance fished the key out of her purse. Instead of unlocking the heavy slab door, however, she deliberately aimed for the back corner of the cabin.

"Oh, but Mr. Henning, you simply must see the creek and the bridge first," she insisted, her voice saccharine-sweet. "The owner herself insists. It's positively charming back here."

He scowled and lingered in front of the door, his face exasperated. He tapped his watch.

Tap it till it cracks, Constance thought, willing away her attraction to him. I don't live in your pocket.

"Nonsense, Mr. Henning, you can see them from here. I promise, you won't miss your plane *or* muss your shoes."

If he felt the barb she'd just thrust into him, Constance couldn't tell it. He gave up and headed toward her. She wasn't sure if he was simply limping, or limping and trying to cover it.

"Look at that! Dead of winter, yet the fox grapes and wild mint are flourishing back here," she pointed out. "The mint makes a delicious mountain tea."

"How *interesting*," he replied from a stoic dead-pan, mimicking her. His voice sounded machine-generated.

Not bothering to get his permission, Constance walked the short distance to the bridge. She wondered how he could *not* be captivated by the beauty of this spot.

The creek formed a clear little pool beneath the stone arch of the bridge. The water's calm, glassine surface wrinkled with each wind gust. Golden fingers of sunlight poked through the leafless canopy of trees surrounding them. From the bridge she could look straight down and glimpse the silvery flash-and-dart of minnows.

He joined her on the bridge, pointedly ignoring the view. His cool, smoky stare riveted to her.

Why, his face is sweaty, she noted. But it was quite brisk weather up here, practically no humidity. She felt chilly even with her wool blazer, while he had no topcoat at all.

She pointed toward some mossy boulders half-submerged at the water's edge. "Those always put me in mind of green-upholstered stools. Aren't they fascinating?"

His stony silence implied he couldn't care less. Constance noticed how his shadow seemed long and sinister in the waning light. She'd left her sunglasses in the Jeep, and when she looked up at him she was forced to lift a hand to shade her eyes from the low sun.

"Miss Adams," he began, laboring to speak, "I confess I don't give a tinker's damn about those rocks. Now...are you going to unlock that cabin or not?"

Or not? His pointed emphasis on those last two words altered her mood. Suddenly she was fully aware of his intimidating physical advantage over her. She wondered, for just a moment, what might happen if she said *not.* But she decided she didn't want to find out.

"Of course." She gave in, stepping around him and walking down off the bridge. "But to be frank, Mr. Henning, I can't imagine you being very...at home up here. As you can see, this is a nature lover's hideaway. The place isn't even wired for electricity."

"I'll use a portable generator," he replied curtly. "It's just for vacations, anyway."

By now her dislike for this rude, intimidating man made Constance desirous of discouraging him. Like Hazel, she wasn't simply interested in selling the cabin—she wanted to match it up with someone who appreciated its rustic charms. *This* creep would be bored by the Grand Canyon.

She unlocked the heavy padlock, slid it from the hasp, and swung the front door wide open, flooding the dark, musty interior with light.

"Pretty basic," she told him, which was certainly true. The unfurnished cabin was partitioned into two rooms, with a sleeping loft over the largest.

Only a few braided rugs covered the floorboards.

"I need a little more light," he told her, crossing to one of the shuttered windows. He slid it up, slid back the bolt lock on the heavy batten shutters, and swung them wide.

She only wanted to be rid of this man. She stayed back in the doorway, saying nothing to further a sale.

He glanced around indifferently.

"Well," he said after a few moments, adding nothing else. She noticed that his eye coloring was variable according to the light—the smoky tint she noticed outside seemed almost like a teal blue in here. He really was extraordinarily good-looking, if one could see past that sneer of cold command. And that ashen complexion...it seemed curiously unhealthy in light of his robust build.

"Thank you," he told her with another cursory dismissal. "I'll give it some thought and call you."

Despite her desire to be rid of him, Constance could hardly believe her ears. The man had been downright desperate to see the place. But now, clearly, his tone was cold—he had no intention whatsoever of calling her, she could tell.

"Fine, Mr. Henning," she replied with a bare minimum of civility. Never mind her wasted time; at least she'd be rid of him. "Now I really must get back to Mystery."

"Let me close the shutter and window," he offered quickly as she started toward them. She could have sworn his limp seemed more pronounced when he crossed to the window. For the first time, she noticed the small tear in his trousers on the back of the left thigh. A dark stain ringed it. The tear and the stain was at odds with the man's impeccable attire, and she wondered if it had anything to do with the fact that he was in a hurry.

"You forgot to bolt the shutter," she pointed out as he turned to join her.

"No, it's fine," he assured her, his tone brooking no debate on the matter.

She was on the verge of pointing out that it clearly was *not* locked—she could see a seam of daylight where the shutters failed to join tightly.

Then she spotted it on the bare wooden floor, brightly illuminated in the sunlight flooding through the front door: a glistening scarlet drop that could only be fresh blood.

For a long moment she paused, on the edge of her next breath, cold dread filling her limbs as if they were buckets under a tap. She glanced around and spotted another drop, another—several of them, all marking places where he had walked.

A terrible sense of foreboding gripped her. She had to grab hold of the door to steady herself. Henning, meantime, had stepped outside, waiting for her to lock up.

"Mr. Henning?" she said without turning around.

"Yes?"

"Are you...I mean—Mr. Henning, are you... bleeding?"

The moment she asked, some instinct warned her she should have pretended not to notice. His next comment verified her instinct.

"I'm sorry you had to notice that, Miss Adams. I truly wish to God you hadn't."

Fighting a sudden, watery weakness in her calves, she turned toward the yard to confront him. And encountered the single, unblinking eye of the gun in his hand.

Chapter 3

The moment she spotted the gun, Constance felt her heart surge. For a few seconds, an exploding pulse made angry-surf noises in her ears.

He wasn't actually pointing it *at* her, but he certainly hadn't pulled it out for show-and-tell, either.

"I'm sorry, Miss Adams," he repeated. "You're too observant for your own good. It would've been much…simpler if you hadn't noticed those bloodstains."

Maybe it was the influence of too many movies, but the possible significance of his words made her go numb with fright.

That same fear must have addled her reason, she decided, judging from her next comment—which surprised her at least as much as it seemed to surprise him.

"You deceitful *bastard!*" She spat the words at him with a contempt unmitigated by her fear.

Bastard...the word had a B-movie feel in her mouth, yet it came out automatically from the depths of her anger and indignation. If she had been burned by a dishonest fiancé, this was infinitely worse. So far as she knew, Doug had never sunk to the level of holding a gun on someone.

However, even more surprising than her comment was his reaction to it.

The impact on him was visible and startling. Something desperate and frightened flashed in those variable eyes of his. Not anger, precisely, but somehow she had touched a very raw nerve.

"No," he told her. "No. It's..."

His voice trailed off, and he waved his free hand in a dismissive oh-what's-the-use gesture. "It's not what you think," he finished, offering no more.

"Mr. Henning, please, I don't—"

"It's Quinn Loudon, not George Henning."

"Well who*ever* you are, I don't understand. You say it's not what I think it is. I assure you, I don't know *what* to think."

He still stood outside in the newly gathering darkness. Instead of answering her, Loudon cast a nervous glance back toward the road. The temperature was going down with the sun, and she saw him shiver in his business suit.

"Come with me," he told her.

Alarm made her pulse race. "Where...where are we going?"

"Look, just get a grip, would you? We're not going anywhere. I'm not a rapist or a killer, and believe me, I don't want you here any more than you want to be here. Right now I just want to hide the cars behind the cabin, and I want you in my sight while I do it, all right? Do you think both vehicles will fit back there?''

"I really couldn't tell you," she said cautiously. "Hiding cars from the law isn't my specialty."

"Who said I'm hiding anything from the law? Maybe I *am* the law."

She looked at the gun in his hand. "No you're not. You're just a criminal swaggering around like a big man, frightening unarmed women. What's next, a raid on a daycare center?"

Now anger did indeed spark in those compelling eyes of his. But he slipped the gun back into its holster under his jacket.

When she still refused to move outside, he seized her under one elbow and tugged her out into the yard. His grip felt strong as a steel trap and intimidated her into passivity. He could do plenty of damage without a gun, she had to admit to herself with a chill inching down her spine.

"Get in," he ordered her, opening the passenger door of the Jeep.

The moment she did, she remembered the keys were in the ignition. By the time he'd limped around to the driver's door, she had managed to lock both doors and scoot behind the steering wheel.

She keyed the ignition and the engine coughed to life. She ground the gearshift into reverse just a moment before he smashed out the driver's window with the butt of his gun.

She went nowhere. The parking brake held. His hand like a warm vise pressed into her throat.

"*Don't* test me," he growled in a low, rough voice. "I'm a very desperate man, Miss Adams."

Only one question looped through her mind: Would he really hurt her?

One part of her didn't think so—some things about him just didn't seem to tally up as criminal—a violent criminal, at any rate. His speech, for one thing, and his appearance.

Then again, she recalled bitterly, he wouldn't be the first callow man who fooled the decent with good tailoring. Doug, too, had been a natty dresser with impeccable manners. And face it, she admonished herself. He'd played her like a piano.

Closing her eyes, she surrendered the need to fight. The crime playing out now wasn't about credit cards and sweet lies of love. She knew nothing about the man before her. The only thing she did know was that he was at least giving her a warning—something Doug had never done. If she was a fool and underrated the man's evil capacity, she could end up dead. So she had to take heed. She had to.

He leaned one meaty shoulder through the window and took the car keys. She moved over into the passenger's seat as if he burned her.

Noticeably favoring his hurt left leg, he climbed in and drove the Jeep around back. He parked as close to the cabin as he could.

"Should be just enough room for my car," he muttered, thinking out loud, his face lean and pale.

"You're not really an investment advisor, are you?" she asked as he pushed her in front of him as they went around the cabin for his car.

He shook his head. "I'm a lawyer. I'm with the U.S. Attorney's Office out of Billings. Or at least I *was*," he added in a bitter afterthought.

A great cover, she told herself, for a criminal to pose as the law.

On the other hand, she did note he had the serious lawyerly type down pat.

Except for the hole in his leg.

They got into the Lexus and moved it to the rear of the cabin. In the ensuing silence, she finally asked the question she feared she already knew the answer to. "So what's wrong…what happened to you?"

"I was shot," he told her bluntly. "About three, four hours ago. At the courthouse in Kalispell."

She ratcheted up her courage a few more notches and asked, "By whom?"

"I couldn't tell you the gentleman's name. He was one of these rude assholes who shoot you without introducing themselves."

She said nothing. There was no point in tossing back a retort, such as maybe he was shot because he was doing something he shouldn't have. By the tight expression on his face, she wasn't going to get any more information out of him. For right now at least.

When he did finally say something, mostly to end the painful silence between them, he was still evasive.

"I understand how all this must appear to you, but the process of observation defines only one reality. Others you haven't observed are just as real."

"Well, you certainly can *talk* like a lawyer." *Or his guilty client,* she thought pointedly.

He surprised her by smiling, although there was no mirth or playfulness in it. "I suppose I do. But I don't put the noose before the gavel."

He pushed her inside the cabin.

"With those shutters closed it's getting dark in here," he observed. "Any lanterns or anything?"

"Candles, I think," she responded reluctantly. "Try the cabinet near the sink."

He limped over, rummaged in the cabinet, and produced several squat votive candles and a box of kitchen matches. He lit two of the candles, and set both of them on the floor. Then, emitting a weary sigh, he gingerly sat down between the candles and supported his back against the cabinet. She noticed he was shivering again.

She was still holding her purse. She thought about her cell phone, then remembered that someone in her family should be calling her soon to check on her. Her fear, momentarily forgotten while they moved the cars, now returned in full force. The man had shown all the tenderness of a wounded lion. He wouldn't take kindly to any more tricks. Staring at his large form and tough, weary expression, she suddenly realized the truth of the "eighth house." She should have never come up to the mountains and shown the cabin. It had proven disastrous.

"Do you have to pace like that?" he sniped.

"I'm sorry. The gun makes me nervous," she confessed.

"I put it away."

"Yes, but it's right there, handy. Isn't it?"

He ignored her, sleeving beads of sweat off his forehead. His wound was getting worse, she realized when she noticed his pain-clouded eyes. Despite her fear and anger, she felt a twinge of pity for him.

"Who shot you?" she repeated. "The police?"

He shook his head. "Not the same police you have in mind. It was federal marshals."

She halted, shocked into immobility. Federal marshals…his crime or crimes must be serious.

He gave a snort at the look on her face. "If you can't handle the answers, don't ask the questions."

"You needn't worry about what I can handle."

She started pacing again.

"Will you please sit the hell down?" he demanded. "I'm getting a crick in my neck watching you."

"I'll sit down," she agreed, doing so. "Now will you *please* tell me what's going on, Mr. Loudon?"

For some time he simply ignored her question. Finally he nodded. When he spoke, his voice showed the strain he'd been through lately.

"I'll leave out the names and just cut to the chase. Basically, I was sent out here from Washington, D.C., to assist on a massive, ongoing investigation into kickback schemes involving the Montana Department of Highways. Or I guess I should say *allegedly* involving them."

"I've heard the word all my life," she confessed, "but I'm not exactly sure what a 'kickback' is."

"It just means a slice of the pie. Cost overruns are a venerable part of construction profits. You know, the doubling or even tripling of a project's estimated price after the work is underway. Most in government understand this and seldom bring indictments over it. But lately there's been a corps of new, reform-minded attorneys in the Justice Department. We're trying to change the business-as-usual graft."

He hesitated, as if trying to gather his thoughts. The front door stood open, the wedge of sky it revealed turning purplish blue in twilight. A breeze wafted, making the candles gutter. For a moment Constance smelled the clean, nose-tickling tang of the evergreens on the lower slopes. It only made her more miserable to be his captive.

"One day last spring," he resumed, "I had to go see a certain judge in Billings. It was a touchy matter—I had already, under federal guidelines for internal review, subpoenaed certain phone and financial information on some attorneys he knew on a social basis. I'm allowed to do that, without notifying anyone, so long as no charges are filed."

This time when he hesitated, on a sharp intake of hissing breath, she knew it was his wound.

"Anyway, I intended to ask the judge's permission to execute a search warrant. I wanted agents to seize the private financial records of a certain state legislator, a guy I suspect is at the heart of the kickback scheme."

A spasm of pain crossed his face, etching his handsome features even deeper in the candlelight.

"I never did talk to that judge. The county sheriff and I were on the verge of knocking on his office door when we saw the door was open a crack, and the judge was inside with a…ahh, let's call him an attorney who represents certain road-construction bosses. This attorney was also one of the guys I had been investigating. Right before my ears and eyes— and the sheriff's—he hands a briefcase stuffed with money to the judge."

"A bribe?" she encouraged him to continue when he hesitated.

"The wise guys never use that word. It's usually called a contribution, but damn straight it was a bribe. I knew it and the sheriff knew it. Schra—I mean, this judge regularly rules on cases involving the attorney's clients."

He paused, and she watched him touch a dry tongue to chapped lips. "Does that thing work?" he asked her, pointing to the hand pump bolted to the sideboard of the sink.

"I think so. It's cistern water, but up here it's safe to drink."

She resisted the urge to help him when he struggled to his feet. He pumped the air out of the pipes, then waited for the rusty water to run clear. She watched him cup his hand and drink greedily.

"Anyway," he said, picking up the thread of his story again as he joined her on the floor, "I made one very stupid mistake. I forgot all about the hallway security cameras that are standard equipment now in courthouse buildings. The tapes are routinely reviewed, at fast speed, and any unusual events are reported. So there the sheriff and I were, caught on film outside the judge's door. And of course the date and time were recorded, too."

"I see. So the men who were inside had sure knowledge that you came to the door and saw them?"

He nodded, his face morose and pensive in that flickering, yellow-orange light.

"Exactly. At first I thought it was just the security cameras that might have them worried. Us standing outside the door when the bribe came down. But now the sheriff's missing. And I realize they must know, or at least suspect, that I've been building a case against them. They've turned my own game against me."

"How do you know?"

His voice was sharp with bitter resentment. "The sheriff was just a good old boy retired from the fed that I knew and liked. We had lunch whenever we both had to go to the courthouse. He had nothing to do with the situation, just the wrong place, wrong time. Now he's missing.'' He stared at her, his eyes dark and sunken in his pain-filled face. ''When they realized what we saw they knew it'd be damn hard to off an assistant U.S. Attorney in the middle of an investigation, but Cod—I mean, the sheriff, he was a piece of cake. They made him disappear, then they set about turning all the evidence against me, even that tape. You see, *I* was carrying a briefcase, too. So it was totally logical to simply suggest that I had come by that day to bribe the judge. Then, seeing he was with someone, I supposedly changed my mind and left without knocking.''

''But how could they prove such a charge from that tape?'' she asked, incredulous.

''They couldn't, of course. But the judge swore out a deposition that I tried to bribe him soon after that. So the tape became corroborative evidence, one more nail in my coffin. And believe me, they've planted far more incriminating evidence against me since then. The newfound cash in my apartment in Washington was why I had to escape today.''

He fell silent, evidently exhausted by the effort to tell her all this. Then Constance noticed the fresh bloodstain growing under his leg. His wound was bleeding again.

Looking at his haggard features, it occurred to her for the first time. He just might not make it.

It might mean her own salvation. If he died, she could escape.

But gazing closer into his pain-filmed eyes, she felt a deep sympathy well up inside her. Despite his holding a gun on her, despite everything she'd suffered because of Doug's treachery, Loudon made her want to believe him. He had an earnestness that was hard to look away from, and his story was related in such a fashion that it didn't make sense to her he'd use his last strength to tell her lies. There was no purpose to any lies now. She was still his unwilling prisoner.

However, neither could she forget Hazel's remark about Doug: *Even the devil can cite Scripture for his purpose.*

His voice suddenly sliced into her thoughts.

"Here," he told her, handing her a black leather wallet.

The wallet was opened to a photo ID that bore the official seal of the U.S. Justice Department. It identified Quinn Loudon as an assistant U.S. Attorney.

"I believe who and what you are," she told him carefully, handing it back.

"But anyone can turn rotten, right? Is that what you're implying?"

"You're bleeding," she pointed out, sidestepping his question. But in fact he'd hit the proverbial nail right on the head—"good guys" were not guaranteed by badges and IDs. The headlines proved, every day, that good guys became bad guys for the right price.

Loudon pulled his shirttails out and ripped off a strip of the material. Quickly he folded it into a makeshift bandage.

"Turn your head," he ordered her.

When she hesitated, he simply shrugged. "Suit yourself, I'm not bashful."

When she heard his belt buckle clinking and realized he was lowering his trousers, she did quickly turn away while he tied the cloth around his wound.

"All right," he told her a few moments later. "Peep show's over."

"You've got to get to a doctor," she told him. "That wound could infect."

"Nix on that. By law doctors have to report every gunshot wound. I've already figured out what I need to do first. I've got one possible ace in the hole, but I'll need to drive to Billings if I mean to play it."

"That's a 400-mile drive," she reminded him. "You'll never make it."

"Probably not," he agreed. "That's why you're going to take me. And we'll need to use your vehicle. By now mine has to be the object of a state-wide search."

"No," she said. "I'm afraid. I...your story is quite convincing. But it's only your word. Besides, even if I chose to believe you—this is obviously a very serious situation. I just...I can't, I'm sorry. I'm just too afraid."

"I don't recall *asking* you," he reminded her, and a sinister tone of menace had entered his voice—or so it seemed to her in her fright.

"I can't," she insisted.

"Yes, you can."

"All right then, I *won't*."

"Actually, it's best that you refuse. That way you don't become an accessory or get charged with aiding and abetting a fugitive. It's this that will force you, and that's what you'll tell the authorities later."

His hand slipped inside his suit jacket and emerged with the gun. Again he didn't aim it at her—but he held it in plain view as a reminder.

"You *will* drive me to Billings, Miss Adams." His stare pierced her. "End of discussion."

I'm in deep, thought Quinn, and going deeper. Despite the long drink in the cabin, the inside of his mouth tasted as dry and stale as the last cracker at the bottom of the barrel. He hadn't eaten all day, and his pinched stomach felt like it had been pumped.

Additionally, even the black plastic bag covering the smashed window didn't entirely keep out the cold. Constance Adams's Jeep did not ride nearly so smoothly as his Lexus. Each time it bounced over a hole or rut on Old Mill Road, pain exploded in his thigh. But even at its worst, the physical pain was nothing compared to his inner turmoil.

His criminal actions earlier today, in Kalispell, while certainly censurable could at least be partially defended. They had caught him completely flat-footed, unprepared, and he simply reacted in a panic. After all, his freedom was on the line. He had been fighting the threat of wrongful imprisonment as well as ensuring his ability to disprove the phony charges against him.

But now…now it was a whole new criminal ball game. He had taken a hostage under the implied threat of violence. Only sheer desperation could have driven him to such an action. "Beyond the pale" hardly described his conduct now.

The heater was blowing, and he wasn't shivering now. He opened the passenger's window to let the cold night air revive him a bit. A sliver of nascent moon hung over the serrated mountain peaks, golden against a blue-black evening sky.

Constance Adams had said nothing during the ride back down to the valley floor and the interstate highway. Now she finally spoke up.

"Mr. Loudon? If you really are innocent, as you say, you should easily be able to clear yourself, shouldn't you? Won't your actions now just make things needlessly worse for you?"

"Easily? Believe me, given the men I'm up against, it would be *easier* to write my name on water."

There was so much more to it, he thought in a welter of despair and misery, that she just couldn't understand from outside the situation. The money planted in his apartment back east, for example. He realized now that this scam involved more players than just Whitaker and Schrader. Others were involved, and there was some sort of *sub-rosa* accord between them.

Quinn wished he *could* make her understand the enormity and complexity of his situation. He hardly knew the woman, but something about her made him believe she could be a strong ally if he could somehow win her trust.

Something else suddenly occurred to him, and a prickle of alarm moved down his spine.

"Do you have a road map of Montana?" he demanded.

"In the glovebox, I think. But we won't need it. I've driven to Billings plenty of times."

"Yeah, on the interstate," he replied as he opened the accordion folds of the map. "But do you know the back roads?"

"You mean all the way to Billings? No. Why take back roads? We aren't in your car."

He flicked on the dome light to study the map. "I just realized there'll probably be an APB out on me. Checkpoints will be set up along the main routes. I can't risk it."

"You really think it's that important to the police?"

"You kidding? I fired on federal agents. They'll raise six sorts of hell."

"You *fired* at them?"

"What, you think they shot me because they don't like my face?"

"You didn't tell me...I mean...."

She trailed off, too taken aback to speak. He could feel a new level of tension in the Jeep.

"If it makes any difference," he told her, "I didn't exactly fire *at* them. I fired deliberately high to miss them."

While the overhead light was on, he felt her glance keep touching him, then quickly sliding away. Even mired in pain and worry, he couldn't help appreciating her good looks. Understandably, this latest revelation had left her somewhat whey-faced. But she had stunning amber eyes and medium-length hair the color of burnt sienna. The only feature even slightly out of harmony with the serenity of her face were her somewhat witchy eyebrows. But he liked them. Liked them a lot. She was the kind of woman who looked liked she could play angel or devil depending on her mood. In truth, if they'd met under any other circumstances, he'd have let her known without a doubt he was attracted to her.

But he had other worries now. Big ones. He quickly worked out a route, along secondary roads, that would be safer but considerably longer. He turned the light out just before Old Mill Road—smooth blacktop now—leveled out on the floor of Mystery Valley.

"Just go on past the interstate," he directed her. "Take County Line Road east."

He sat back in the seat and allowed his ruminations to turn toward the situation at hand. Despite all that had happened to him, Quinn couldn't really say he was surprised by what Schrader and Whitaker were up to. They were corrupt, and greed was a powerful motivator.

He wasn't sure, however, about prosecutor Dolph Merriday. True, the man had real facility with a cliché—scratch a federal prosecutor and you'll find an ambitious politician. But something bothered Quinn about the man. Above all, prosecutors were negotiators. But his unyielding stance...

Constance Adams abruptly interrupted his ruminations.

"Mr. Loudon?" She looked at him from the wheel, hesitating, thinking, her pretty lips curved down. "If—if your story is true, then I know you don't want to become a real criminal by kidnapping me. There's a state-trooper post ahead at Oxbow. You can turn yourself in there, and if you do, I promise you I'll press no charges. We'll call this a lift."

He greeted her suggestion with a harsh bark of laughter. "And will you give me a lollipop, too, Miss Goody Two-Shoes?"

After that dig, he could almost whiff the anger coming off her.

"Why is it such a joke?" she demanded. "You could avoid kidnapping charges—"

"I can't," he cut her off tersely. "You've watched too many crime shows on TV where crusading lawyers always ensure that justice prevails. In real life innocent people are framed all the time."

"So your rights are more important than mine, is that it? Why should *I* be victimized because you supposedly were?"

"Curiosity killed the cat, that's why. All you had to do was keep your mouth shut when you saw that blood on the floor. The unlocked shutter didn't give me away—the blood did. Once I knew you'd seen it, I also knew you'd report me."

"I see. I'm being punished for showing a little concern."

"I don't want to punish you." The truth of his words stabbed him and forced him to grow silent. With difficulty, he added, "But things are the way they are, that's all. Now just shut up and drive."

"Please let me stop at Oxbow," she repeated, her voice pleading. "I know you don't want to become a common criminal."

"Look," he answered harshly, his patience worn by the pain of his leg, and the pain in his soul, "I'll keep it to a simple command—shut your damned mouth and drive."

He noticed she had been checking her watch every few minutes. She did so again now.

"Got a hot date?" he asked her.

"What if I did? Doesn't really matter, does it? My time is yours now—gun man," she added pointedly.

Her words cut far deeper than she realized.

He sank farther down into the seat and morosely surveyed the situation. Ms. Constance Adams would never know how hard it all sat with him. He'd spent his childhood in a series of foster homes after his real parents—both of them drug addicts—had gone to prison for holding up a liquor store to support their habit.

His last foster home had been the best—police Lieutenant Jim Westphal and his wife Ceil had loved him like their own son. From Jim, Quinn had caught the crime-fighting bug. He geared his whole life toward a career in law enforcement. He wanted, more than anything else, to be one of the good guys in the war on crime. As if only that could erase all the pain and humiliation his real parents had caused him.

And now, as if there were some kind of dark, blood destiny coursing through his veins, he, too, was officially a criminal. Certainly he would never hurt this woman whom he held against her will; violence, at least, was not in him. She had no idea that his gun was empty and he had no more bullets for it. Somehow it had been easier to bluff with an empty weapon—he could never have pointed a loaded gun at her.

But the thought was little consolation. With every mile they drove, he sank deeper and deeper into anguish. It just didn't seem possible that fate could be so cruel—could in fact force him into the very role he'd fought his entire life to avoid.

Again he noticed her nervously check her watch. He opened his mouth to ask her about it again. But before he could speak, a telephone chirred, the sound muffled by her purse.

Someone was calling for her.

Chapter 4

The phone rang a second time, a third. With every ring, Constance could feel her body stiffen. The ache to grab it and scream for help was smothered by the fear of the gun in Loudon's pocket. Every ring was torture.

It was Beth Ann, or someone else in her family, checking up on her as she'd requested. By now they would have already called her house, too. Obviously, Constance told herself, the only option was not to answer. That alone would set her family in motion trying to find her.

But she underestimated her captor's shrewdness. He evidently didn't trust her complacency.

"Answer it," he ordered her.

At the same time he grabbed the steering wheel with one hand.

He spoke quickly. "I know you figure by now that I won't shoot you. You're right about that. But I swear by all things holy—you send *even one hint* to that caller, and I'll dump both of us into that ditch just like *that.*''

Steep runoff ditches ran along both sides of the road, and the Jeep was moving at fifty-five miles per hour. She knew he could well be bluffing. But he jerked the wheel to warn her, and her heart missed a beat when they nearly swerved into the ditch.

''Answer it,'' he ordered tersely as the phone continued to burr. ''And no tricks.''

She fished the cell phone out of her purse. Loudon leaned his head close to hers, listening in.

''Hello?''

''God, 'bout time you answered, pokey,'' Beth Ann's voice complained. ''What took you so long?''

When Constance hesitated, Loudon again jerked the wheel. The Jeep's tires spewed gravel when they brushed the narrow shoulder. She felt her throat tighten with fear.

''I was passing two logging trucks,'' she ad-libbed. ''I had to wait until I got around them.''

''Oh. How'd it go? Did the guy buy the old Hupenbecker place?''

''He's still debating, I guess.''

''Sure took you long enough. Is he cute?''

The Jeep hit a slight dip, and Loudon's cheek brushed hers. She felt the rough masculine feel of his beard shadow. She forced herself to keep her tone light.

''Boys are cute, little sis. Men are handsome.''

''Well, is he handsome?''

''Can't say,'' Constance replied reluctantly but truthfully.

''Woo-woo! Are you still there with him?''

Constance took a sideways glance at Loudon. He shook his head and mouthed the word, no.

"No," Connie whispered.

"Can't hear you! We must have a bad connection." Fuzz backed up Beth Ann's assessment. "Well, at least the guy wasn't an ax murderer. I gotta go now. I'm baby-sitting for the Campbells. Later, skater."

Constance felt her heart sink as she put the phone away. If anything did happen to her, it was Friday and no one would be likely to seriously worry about her absence until Monday when her business associate, Ginny Lavoy, would miss her.

Another hazard, she thought bitterly, of having no love life. There was no one to miss you right away.

"'Can't say,'" Loudon repeated, a trace of whimsy mixed with his exhausted tone. "That's a left-handed compliment if I ever heard one."

"I didn't mean to give you even a left-handed one," she said, dead hope in her voice.

Loudon smirked and checked his watch. "Bad news travels fast," he told her, turning on the radio to catch the top-of-the-hour news broadcast out of Helena.

The national news came first, the usual litany of political squabbling and natural-disaster news caused by abnormally warm ocean currents. Then the announcer turned to state news.

"The sound of gunfire erupted today at the Federal Court Building in Kalispell. Quinn Loudon, Assistant U.S. Attorney, literally blasted his way to freedom when U.S. Marshals attempted to place him under arrest. Loudon had appeared for pretrial proceedings stemming from charges of bribery and racketeering.

"According to witnesses, during the exchange of fire Loudon was wounded in one leg. He successfully eluded officials and escaped from Kalispell. A massive manhunt is presently underway, according to federal prosecutor Dolph Merriday.

"'Quinn Loudon has lived a life of deceit,'" Merriday told reporters during a press conference only hours ago, 'so today's actions are no real surprise.' According to Merriday, even Loudon's superiors at the Justice Department did not realize Loudon's parents were both career criminals who served long prison sentences.

"'We caught him in the act, so he blasted up a courthouse to get free,' Merriday added. 'But his kind always foul their nests sooner or later.'"

The story was over in thirty seconds and the announcer moved on to other news. Constance felt a sudden numbness at the mention of Loudon's criminal parents. While nothing in the news story actually contradicted anything he had told her, it lent an official—and damning—authority to the notion that he was a very dangerous felon.

Loudon turned the radio off, cursing softly.

"Well that flat does it," he declared bitterly. "The bastards broke the knife off in me this time."

Flat does *what,* she wondered, frightened by the desperation in his tone.

Loudon lapsed into a brooding silence.

Lance Pollard was right, he told himself. The case against him was indeed all smoke and mirrors.

Unfortunately, a cynical proverb he'd learned in law school was also true: *No one ever went broke underestimating the intelligence of the American people.* Smoke and mirrors were enough to convict a man. Well, no doubt Schrader and Whitaker were dancing on his grave already. But damn them, anyway. He wasn't in it just yet.

Constance had said nothing. Now, as he fell quiet, the awkward silence became unbearable.

"Now, at least, I understand your steamroller methods," she told him. "This is obviously a very big deal if it led the state news."

"I know what you're thinking. There were two unpleasant details I left out of my story to you. Two details called my mother and father."

The bitterness and hurt in his voice made her think of the pain Doug Huntington had caused her. What if *she* had been branded a criminal because she slept with one?

"Since when did children get automatic criminal status from their parents?" she asked coolly.

"They don't. It was a cheap shot by Merriday."

"Yes. And besides, you deserve credit for having done a lot in the criminal world all by yourself."

He flinched. Then he almost laughed. "You are one difficult woman. And your damned sense of fair play only makes what I'm doing right now that much more reprehensible. Truly I'm sorry, Miss Adams, I really am. I just...I had no choice but to drag you into this. They didn't mention on the radio that Sheriff Cody Anders is missing either. I don't want to go missing like he did, so it's got to be this way."

"I'm sorry," she whispered bitterly, not looking at him.

"You still don't believe me, right?" he pushed.

"No," she admitted.

After a long silence, he replied inexplicably, "Good girl. You didn't even know me until a little while ago.'' His voice almost seemed to be fading like a weak radio signal.

They passed through the bright glow of a yard light, and she noticed the haggard pockets under his eyes.

He's exhausted, she thought, and he's probably lost a lot of blood.

Even as she felt pity welling inside her, a more practical side of her warned against it. Ask every convict in a prison, and he'll swear he's innocent, she reminded herself. This was not a field trip they were on; she was his unwilling hostage.

He lapsed into silence, either dozing or close to it. She watched the blacktop streak past under the headlight beams, trying not to dwell on Dolph Merriday's troubling words: *Quinn Loudon has lived a life of deceit.*

Constance wasn't sure how long her passenger had dozed. She suddenly started when his voice abruptly ended the quiet inside the Jeep.

''Where are we?''

''About ten miles west of Bighorn Falls.''

''Is that all?'' he complained.

''I'm driving the nighttime speed limit. Would you like me to go faster?''

''No,'' he said irritably. Montana state troopers were notoriously vigilant after dark.

''You insisted on taking the back roads to Billings,'' she reminded him. ''This route is far less direct.''

''I know what I said,'' he snapped at her.

He was awake, but his voice sounded exhausted. Something occurred to her.

"Have you eaten anything today?"

"No, but we can't stop anywhere. I can't risk it."

"There's a few granola bars in the glovebox," she told him.

He handed her one, too, and they both ate in silence for a few minutes.

Constance was the first to break it.

"You mentioned something about having an 'ace in the hole' in Billings. May I ask what it is?"

When he answered, his voice had lost its snappish tone. "I'd better not get too specific with you. You'll be going to the police eventually. And you may end up being grilled by the same goons who're trying to put handles on me."

"I take your point."

"Now you're catching on. Actually I doubt if what I have is an ace. But with luck, maybe it'll turn out to be a king or a jack. So far it's my secret. All on my own, I was putting together a case against…the two men who are trying to set me up. I kept my efforts secret because I was afraid to jeopardize security until I have some idea just how high up the corruption goes."

Quinn thought about how one secretly obtained court order had allowed him to painstakingly assemble a damning paper trail from phone and financial records. As huge amounts of money were released from the Federal Highway Fund to a major Montana road-construction firm, he had traced subsequent "portfolio diversifications" by the firm's attorney— Brandon Whitaker.

Over time a clear pattern emerged. So regular you could plot it like a graph. A pattern known as "the kickback curve'' among prosecutors. After each federal payment to Montana, Whitaker initiated lucrative transactions involving preferred stocks and leveraged buyouts. It was only circumstantial. But it would warrant judicial examination; Quinn was sure of that.

Despite her resolution to remain skeptical, Constance again felt herself wanting to believe her abductor. True, he was holding back specific details. But ever since their paths had crossed earlier, he had insisted on his innocence.

He didn't really need to bother doing that—he had a gun, after all. A true criminal would simply rely on intimidation to gain her compliance.

Once again he lapsed into a long silence. His labored breathing became more obvious to her as he nodded out once more. Before long, his head had slumped onto her shoulder.

No question about it now; he was fast asleep. She glanced down. The greenish glow of the dashboard lights showed that his coat was open.

I could maybe get the gun, she thought.

But then what? She knew full well she wouldn't use it, and he probably knew that, too.

She thought about her cell phone. Had he been thinking like a real bad guy, he would have taken it from her. But he didn't. She could get it out, dial 911, and perhaps whisper to the emergency operator. Give their location and let the police take it from there.

Yet, she made no move to try. It wasn't just fear he'd wake up and catch her. As much as she hated to admit it, she was starting to see this mess from his perspective, too.

If he *was* innocent—a strong possibility in her mind—then she might be condemning him to prison—or worse. If he were simply running to get away, Billings was the last place he'd head for. From frontier days to the present, Montana fugitives chose the Canadian Rockies to the north as their favorite refuge from the law.

Even as all this looped through her mind, a blue-and-yellow sedan eased by her in the passing lane—a Montana state trooper.

Her pulse leapt into her throat. The cop wasn't pulling her over, just passing on his way to someplace else.

Flick the bright lights on and off a few times, she thought. That cop will pull you right over.

And then what? Loudon was armed and desperate—this time he might not aim high.

Wracked by indecision, she did nothing as the red-glowing taillights receded ahead.

She assumed Loudon was sound asleep. So hearing his voice made her nearly crawl out of her skin.

"Missed your chance," he told her in a sleepy voice. "S'matter, you soft on crime?"

"Maybe I don't want to get caught in the middle of one of your shootouts."

"Oh. Here I thought maybe it was my sexy eyes."

Heat came into her face. "I could floor it and still catch that cop."

"You're the driver."

Despite his exhaustion, she detected a smug, mocking tone to his voice. He had called her bluff. It wasn't bad enough that he had kidnapped her—now he had to toy with her to amuse himself.

"Since you're awake, kindly remove your head from my shoulder."

He complied, slumping against the passenger's window.

"Do you know how nice you smell?" he murmured sleepily. "Your perfume is Gardenia Passion, right?"

He was right, but she said nothing. He didn't even wait for a reply, going back to sleep immediately.

She stared ahead at the glowing pinpoints of the trooper's taillights. If she did want to catch him, this was her last chance.

Her anger notwithstanding, she held the Jeep at a steady 55 m.p.h.

Another twenty or so miles rolled past, and Quinn Loudon's breathing became ragged and uneven. Constance took one hand off the wheel to touch the seat near his left thigh.

A prickle of alarm jolted through her when her fingertips came away wet and sticky with blood.

"Mr. Loudon! Mr. Loudon, wake up!"

"Hunh?"

He twitched awake, one hand automatically starting toward his gun.

"What? What's wrong?"

"It's you, that's what wrong. You're bleeding again. And you sound just awful. You need medical help."

"No. Just keep driving."

"Look, these back roads wind all over the place. We aren't even a quarter of the way to Billings. You'll never make it."

"I have to make it."

"No," she insisted firmly. "I am finally rebelling. I will *not* assist you in killing yourself. There's lights up ahead. I'm pulling over and finding out where the nearest doctor or hospital is.''

She braced herself for his next strong-arm tactic. But he surprised her.

''All right,'' he agreed in a flat tone that should have warned her. But in her agitation, she missed the clue.

Up ahead lights blazed a halo around what turned out to be a little crossroads service center—a motel, an all-night diner, a gas station.

''The motel clerk can probably help us,'' she said as she turned onto an apron of gravel in front of the motel. It was one of a dying breed of mom-and-pop independents, a run-down establishment called Sleepy Pete's Motor Inn. An ancient neon VACANCY sign winked on and off like a lighthouse beacon.

''I'll be right back out,'' she promised as she reached to turn off the ignition.

His steel-trap grip stopped her hand.

''Just leave it running and get out,'' he told her.

''What?''

''Lady, I'm weak but not incoherent. You heard me. Look, I appreciate your concern. But leave the Jeep running and get out.''

Plenty of light washed over them now—harsh, anemic light that made his haggard and pale face seem almost cadaverous.

''You're stealing my car?''

''In for a penny, in for a pound. I've fired on feds and kidnapped you all in one day. Why balk now at grand-theft auto?''

He took several bills from his wallet and thrust them at her. ''Here. I can't pay for the Jeep, but I can at least cover your room and a hot meal.''

"I don't need money. I need my vehicle!"

"Why is it always about you?" he joked brusquely. "Now *get*."

Summoning whatever reserves of strength he still possessed, he climbed over the gearshift knob and bodily forced her from her seat.

"Right when I start to feel sorry for you," she spat at him angrily, "you have to show your true colors all over again."

Instantly, even as angry as she felt, she regretted that "true colors" remark. His eyes met hers, and beyond the blurred focus caused by pain she could detect a deep well of hurt—she, too, was accusing him of hereditary evil, just as Dolph Merriday had done by way of the radio.

But there was no time for regrets or apologies. He pushed her roughly away from the driver's door.

"Auf Wiedersehen, fraulein," he said in a weary voice, tossing her a two-finger salute. Then he shut the driver's door and put the transmission in reverse. Only seconds later he was back on the road, taillights receding in the night.

For perhaps a full minute Constance just stood there, staring after him. Her anger receded quickly, replaced by a numb confusion—she didn't know *what* to feel now.

He can't make it, she thought. Even if he really did have some important evidence in Billings, he couldn't make it.

She gradually became aware that she was chilled. Even though the winter night was unseasonably mild, she needed at least a sweater. Clutching her elbows against the cold, she turned and headed reluctantly toward the motel.

From the outside, Sleepy Pete's Motor Inn featured a 1950s motif best described as Luau Gothic. But the interior, she realized the moment she stepped into the front office, was a surprisingly authentic throwback to the nineteenth century.

Reproductions of Currier and Ives color prints adorned the walls, alternating with portraits in gilt-wood frames of prominent Montanans from the frontier days. The old-fashioned lamps had milky glass shades. There were even brass cuspidors in the corners.

The night clerk was a taciturn old man who looked to be straight out of *Genesis*. She signed the register and paid in advance with a credit card. He gave her a room key and a remote for the television.

Constance knew, of course, that she had to call the police. But once in her cramped, mildew-smelling room, she began pacing, occasionally staring at the telephone on its battered nightstand.

She couldn't understand what she was feeling right now. After all the pain Doug's duplicity had caused her, she ought to hate Quinn Loudon. Or if *hate* was too strong, at least despise him.

Instead, she actually felt that she was somehow on the verge of betraying him. She could still see the hurt in his eyes when she alluded to his "true colors."

"This is stupid," she said out loud, addressing her own image in the narrow mirror above a battered oak chiffonnier. "Stupid, stupid, *stupid*." The man was a dangerous criminal, for God's sake. She should be unspeakably relieved he let her go with her life.

But…

Her expression darkened in the reflection.

With resolve she didn't feel, she crossed back to-

ward the phone. She finally noticed the varnished oil
painting on the wall and recognized the beard-
grizzled face immediately. It was Jake McCallum,
Hazel's great-great-grandfather, founder of her world-
famous Lazy M ranch in Mystery Valley.

Jake, too, had the distinct prussian-blue eyes that
lived on in Hazel. As Constance stared into them,
Hazel's words from earlier today whispered in memory: *Does one bad burn mean you must remain in the
cold forever?*

Steeling herself, she turned her back on Jake and
picked up the telephone.

Chapter 5

As it turned out, the dreaded ordeal Constance anticipated from the Montana State Troopers never materialized.

They did respond to her call immediately, of course. But she merely told her story to a polite, professional, plainclothes detective whose interview lasted less than thirty minutes. He even kindly arranged for a rental car to be delivered to the motel so she could drive home next day.

Somehow, though, it all seemed too easy.

She went to bed that night with a strong sense of foreboding. Even calling her parents had left her feeling strange. She'd wanted to tell them everything, but instead found herself holding back. It was as if she didn't want to fully admit a crime had taken place. Somehow she had an inexplicable need to keep the details to herself for a while, as if she still needed to sort out bad from good.

She passed a fitful night in the lumpy bed, dreaming she was back in the Jeep with Quinn Loudon. But with the cartoon logic of dreams, Loudon's face would transform into Doug's.

"Miss Adams? Miss Adams, are you in there?"

Someone's insistent banging on the motel room door startled her awake on Saturday morning. She sat up suddenly, heart thudding, and glanced at the digital clock on the nightstand: just past 7:00 a.m.

"Who is it?" she challenged.

"Miss Adams, my name is Roger Ulrick," responded a voice she instantly disliked. "I'm the assistant district attorney out of Kalispell. I need to ask you some questions about Quinn Loudon."

"Just a minute," she called out, flustered and irritated. She hated wearing the same clothes two days in a row, yet she had no choice but to don her wool skirt and blazer again. At least she had been able to take a long shower the night before. She hurriedly ran a brush through her sleep-tangled hair, trying to ignore the puffy circles around her eyes.

She slid the chain back on the night latch and opened the door. Two men stood waiting in the chill, their breath ghosting.

"Miss Adams, this is Todd Mumford," Ulrick said in a self-satisfied voice that irked her. "He's with the FBI District Office in Billings. May we come in?"

As if I really have any choice, she fumed. But she forced an uncertain smile onto her face. "Yes, of course."

Ulrick offered his hand, which felt warm and gummy in hers. Then he removed his cashmere topcoat and folded it neatly over his arm. He was in his forties, thin and slope-shouldered, dressed in a sagging brown suit and cap-toe Oxfords. She did a double-take at Mumford; the baby-faced, bifocaled agent reminded her of one of those teenagers who used to appear on TV game shows and win big money for being so cerebral.

"I told my story last night to the state troopers," she explained as the two men stepped inside.

"Yes, we know you did," Ulrick confirmed. His intense, probing stare and skeptical smirk seemed more appropriate to an Inquisitor General. "We are required to conduct our own questioning."

"I see," she replied, not really seeing at all.

Mumford was peering all around the room as if he expected to find an exotic bordello. Despite his fashionable blue suit, something about the youthful agent struck her as decidedly old-fashioned. Then she realized: It was his neat, shellacked hair, which had a part straight as a pike.

Ulrick produced a handheld tape recorder and thumbed it on. He asked many of the same questions the detective had asked her last night. Except that he placed far more emphasis on exactly what Loudon told her as well as his precise purpose for wanting to go to Billings.

"Can you elaborate somewhat on his statement that he has an 'ace in the hole?'," Ulrick pressed for the second time.

Constance felt her patience stretching thin. "Do you want me to make something up, Mr. Ulrick? That's all he told me."

Ulrick simply switched to a new line of questioning.

"Did he say exactly where this 'ace' is in Billings?"

She shook her head.

"Miss Adams," he reminded her in a condescending tone, "the tape recorder cannot record a nod."

"No," she snapped back. "He did not tell me where in Billings this ace is being kept."

"Did he say where he might go after he went to Billings?"

So they haven't caught him yet, she inferred. She felt guilty when a weight seemed to lift from her.

"No, he didn't. And frankly, I don't believe he was in any condition to even make it to Billings."

Ulrick's permanent smirk etched itself a bit deeper.

"You sound concerned about that, Miss Adams. Are you?"

"Concerned?"

"Yes. I get the distinct impression it troubles you that he was in need of medical attention. You seem worried about his well-being. That strikes me as...somewhat odd. After all, this man forced you at gunpoint to—"

"Excuse me, Mr. Ulrick," she cut in. "*I* never said he 'forced' me. That's your word, not mine."

Ulrick's long, thin nose wrinkled at the bridge when he frowned.

"I don't understand, Miss Adams. Are you now saying no gun was involved?"

"He had a gun, yes."

"And did he not threaten you with it?"

In her heart, Constance knew the strict answer to that question was probably yes. But by now Ulrick had put her in an adversarial mood.

"Well he *showed* it to me," she stipulated carefully. "And it was a bit threatening, yes."

"*It* was threatening, or *he* was?"

"The gun, I meant."

Ulrick exchanged a long glance with his younger companion. The tape recorder didn't record *that,* either, she thought, keeping the observation to herself.

"Miss Adams," Ulrick lectured her in a patronizing tone, "I'm getting the distinct impression that you are actually sympathetic to your abductor."

"Your impressions are of no interest to me, Mr. Ulrick. And my sympathies are my private business."

"Perhaps. But aiding and abetting a fugitive is the law's business."

Todd Mumford entered the conversation for the first time. His tone was far more reasonable than Ulrick's.

"Miss Adams, federal kidnapping charges are filed automatically whether the victim presses charges or not."

"That's your area of expertise, not mine," she replied curtly. "I'm a Realtor."

"Yes," Ulrick interjected in a pointed tone. "So long as you possess a state license to be one. I assume you know that a felony conviction, in Montana, means revocation of your license?"

Angry blood rushed into her face. "Are you trying to intimidate me, Mr. Ulrick?"

"Merely reminding you of the law, Miss Adams."

"Frankly, I don't believe that's all you're doing. You're treating *me* like a criminal. And you're obviously trying to bully me into giving you information I do not possess."

Ulrick finally lost his smirk as raw anger distorted

his features. But the FBI agent, coolly professional throughout, poured oil on the waters.

"We apologize if our tactics seem a bit high-pressure, Miss Adams. If necessary you would testify in a court of law, would you not?"

"Yes, if absolutely necessary. But only to exactly what I've told you this morning."

Perhaps ten seconds passed in awkward silence as they all pondered the awkward impasse they'd reached. Ulrick, calm again, put his coat back on. Then he folded his arms over his chest and asked one last question.

"Did Loudon give you anything, Miss Adams? Anything at all?"

"Nothing."

"You're sure about that?"

"Mr. Ulrick, which syllable of the word *nothing* are you having trouble understanding? 'No' or 'thing?' Or perhaps you think I'm feebleminded? I believe I would know if somebody gave me something."

Angry blood rushed into Ulrick's face. But Mumford cleared his throat in warning. Ulrick bit back his first, hot-tempered response.

"Sometimes," he informed her primly, "our memory can be affected by our sympathies. For the record, I am noting in my report that you were hostile during this interview. Indeed, I have to wonder just whose side you are on."

"I have no interest in your report. As for my hostility, it is in direct response to your own, Mr. Ulrick. I don't let others push me around. And as to choosing sides—I'm not aware that this is a baseball game. Let me repeat, Loudon gave me *nothing* and did not tell me anything specific about his purpose in going to Billings.''

Ulrick opened his mouth to get in another lick. But Constance didn't give him the chance.

"Now gentlemen, if you will excuse me—this experience has already cost me my vehicle and a day of my time. Unless you plan to place me under arrest, I consider this interview terminated.''

Ulrick obviously resented her assertive manner. But Mumford, forcing back an amused smile, took his companion by the elbow and nudged him toward the door.

Ulrick, however, was not quite finished. He paused to look back at her from the doorway.

"I take it you're returning to Mystery?''

"Yes, this morning. Why do you ask?''

"Because later on we may have more questions for you.''

"What questions that you haven't already asked?''

His lips—the color of raw liver—pursed into an even deeper smirk.

"Frankly, that's our concern, not yours.''

He shut the door, leaving her speechless with anger.

Constance had very little appetite, especially given the foul mood Ulrick had brought on. But she'd had almost nothing to eat since noon yesterday and knew she should try to eat before she drove back to Mystery Valley.

The nearby diner served up a "genuine Western breakfast" special of hot buckwheat cakes, soda biscuits, and sausage gravy—nearly a ton of food, she estimated in dismay when the waitress set down a platter the size of an aircraft carrier's deck.

She gave it a valiant effort, but had to give up after a few bites and settle for two cups of strong black coffee. She walked back to the motel and picked up her rental car keys at the front desk.

"It's the white Ford Taurus right out front," said the young Hispanic woman who had relieved Old Methuselah.

Constance used the three-hour drive back to the valley to mull everything that had happened since last evening, turning each detail over with the fingers of her mind and scrutinizing every facet.

She was not the type who scared easily, and Roger Ulrick's threats about revoking her real-estate license angered her more than they intimidated her. He obviously considered himself pretty high and mighty. And maybe he was. But if she needed it, *she* had an "ace" to play, too—a crusty ace by the name of Hazel McCallum.

The Matriarch of Mystery was also in the thick of Montana politics—one of the quiet power brokers behind the noisy political scene. She was the direct descendent of Jake McCallum, one of the state's earliest pioneers. Thus, she could dial the governor's personal telephone number day or night and be assured of his undivided attention. If Ulrick wanted to play chicken, Constance was sure she could make him blink first.

Gradually her mood softened. It was the gorgeous morning that had a calming effect on her. White-gauze clouds dotted the sky, and even well before noon the winter morning felt like spring. Although the surrounding fields were still winter brown, it was easy to imagine them brilliant with blue columbine and red Indian Paintbrush flowers.

Every now and then her eyes flicked to the rearview mirror. A gray sedan had been behind her for some time now, making no attempt to pass. She thought little of it—the road curved through hill country with few good opportunities to pass.

When she figured that her cell phone was in range for clear conversation, she gave Hazel a call.

"Lazy M ranch," Hazel's deep, throaty voice answered cheerfully. "Chief cook and bottle washer speaking."

"Hi, Hazel, it's Connie."

"Morning, hon. How you doing?"

"You won't believe how I'm doing."

Briefly, Constance recounted the main points of her adventure since calling Hazel yesterday. While she spoke, her eyes cut to the rearview mirror. The gray sedan was still behind her.

"Well, sakes and saints!" Hazel marveled when Constance fell silent. "That Quinn Loudon story was just on the news again this morning. But you weren't mentioned. Matter fact, they said nothing about his taking a hostage."

"Thank God."

She didn't need to tell Hazel the other big reason why she was so grateful—it had been humiliating enough when her former fiancé was arrested. She didn't need to be publicly linked with yet another criminal.

"Evidently Loudon's still on the dodge," Hazel added. "Or so the newscaster reported. And to think he's in your Jeep. Do you have theft insurance?"

"Mm-hmm," she replied absently, feeling a bit

guilty—she hadn't even thought about that. She had worried more about Quinn Loudon than her stolen car. As much as she despised Ulrick, she had to admit he was right. She definitely was "sympathetic" toward Loudon.

She frowned slightly when she checked the mirror again. The gray car stayed well back even though she'd slowed slightly, and on a straight stretch of road where it could easily pass.

"The state trooper told me, last night, that the Feds would be impounding Loudon's car and searching the Hupenbecker cabin immediately. I better drive up there later today—I've got the only key, which means they probably broke the lock. I'll take a new one up there. No telling what kind of condition they left the place in."

"Hon? Would you mind picking me up before you go? I haven't been up there since God was a boy. With the weather like this, it'd be nice to see the old creek and Jake's bridge."

"Would I mind? I'd love to have you along," Constance told her frankly. "Actually, I'm not too eager to go up there alone."

"I don't wonder, poor thing. Just stop by when you're ready. My afternoon is open."

Constance turned the phone off and put it back inside her purse. Two cars and a pickup passed her from behind. But the gray car held its precise distance behind her.

"Hon, *let* them follow us," Hazel scoffed.

Constance wheeled the Ford through the stone gateposts of the Lazy M's long gravel drive.

"Those Feds think they're such a fox-eared tribe,"

Hazel went on. "City whippersnappers, that's all they are. They can't get their cappuccino and croissants up in the mountains. They'll soon get bored with us rural hicks and give it up."

Despite her nervous apprehension, Constance had to smile at Hazel's let-the-devil-take-'em attitude. Very few things could put a ripple in Hazel's calm veneer.

"I don't see the gray car now anyway," Constance remarked. "Maybe they gave up when I went home."

When she glanced in the rearview mirror to check for the sedan, she winced at her reflection.

"I still look like I just rolled out of bed," she carped. "And I've been up for seven hours."

Hazel gave a skeptical snort. "Connie Adams, are you fishing for compliments? A paid-off mortgage doesn't look as pretty as you! All *you* have to do to look good is run a comb through your hair. Good looks are a gift of nature when you're young—they're a carefully constructed illusion for an old roadster like me."

"Now who's fishing?" Constance teased. "If you're an 'old roadster,' Hazel, then you must be a Bentley."

The two friends shared a laugh. The spry seventy-five-year-old coquettishly patted her silver chignon. "I *am* quite devastating, aren't I?"

The afternoon had turned into a beauty, a brilliant ball of sun stuck high in the sky as if pegged there. Hazel's Lazy M cattle ranch occupied the exact center of verdant Mystery Valley, several thousand choice acres of lush pasture criss-crossed by creeks and run-off streams.

"This Quinn Loudon fellow," Hazel remarked,

"has evidently dropped off the face of the earth. I caught the latest news just before you came over. They flashed a photo of him on the screen. You didn't tell me he was such a looker."

"We weren't exactly on a date," Constance quipped wryly. But her face sobered when she added, "So he's still missing?"

"Connie, he must be running like a river when the snow melts. He's still at large in spite of a three-state dragnet. Even the Royal Mounties have been alerted in Alberta and Saskatchewan. I'd say he must be a resourceful young man. That, or else maybe he's bled to death somewhere."

At these last words, a jolt of dread shot through Constance. Something in her face must have given away her concern—she could feel Hazel's shrewd gaze studying her.

"From everything you've told me," Hazel added, "this young man doesn't sound like an out-and-out criminal. He puts me in mind of those wild young fools folks around here used to call 'harum-scarum'— more wild and reckless than criminal. The way A. J. Clayburn used to be before I got him and—"

Hazel caught herself just in time. "I mean, before Jacquelyn Rousseaux tamed him and got him good and married."

Any other time Constance might have grinned at Hazel's slip. For some time she had suspected the crafty old dame of secretly engineering the marriage of rodeo star A.J. and *Mystery Gazette* reporter Jacquelyn.

But for some reason, Hazel's comment about "harum-scarum" men made her recall her careless remark to Loudon, the one about how his "true colors" were showing.

"It's the strangest thing," she confessed to Hazel. "I mean, Quinn Loudon wronged *me*. My God, he even stole my Jeep! Yet…somehow I feel that it's just the opposite. That somehow *I* was unfair to him."

"Face it, girl," Hazel assured her. "We both know that men are good at sailing under false colors. Look how Doug Huntington bamboozled both of us. I dang near ordered you to go out with him, remember? Still…now and again one comes along with a good reason for being tricky."

Hazel's tone, for that final remark, made Constance give her a searching look. Hazel's brisk and cheerful eagerness to face the future could inspire others half her age. But there was also a shrewd nature lurking behind her homespun manner and weather-lined face. She could be crafty, sly, or manipulative as any given situation demanded.

However, the wily widow dropped the topic of Quinn Loudon and poked her head out the window to breathe deeply of the fragrant air.

"Look at those dogwood trees!" she said enthusiastically. "Weather's tricked them. They're swollen with new sap. My soul alive, you couldn't put a price on a day like this."

They entered the town limits of Mystery. With a year-round population of 4,000—swelling to almost twice that by late summer—Mystery was only a fifteen-minute drive due east from the Lazy M. The two blocks comprising the old downtown area still included plenty of its original red-brick buildings with black iron shutters—nothing fancy, just practical and sturdy. But the ornate, nineteenth century opera house with its scrollwork dome had once put the community a cut above plain old saloon towns. So had the stately old courthouse, now the community center and the only gray masonry building in town.

"There's Paul Robeck," Hazel remarked, waving at a tall, well-dressed man coming out of Omenset-ter's Pharmacy. "I buy all my insurance through him. I can't believe he's still single. Handsome, steady, good sense of humor."

She sent Constance a sly sideways glance. "He manages to work your name into every conversation we have, too. I keep telling him, land sakes, Paul, just give the gal a call."

"He has. Several times, actually."

"And...?"

"Oh, Hazel, it's just not a good time for me to start...socializing with men. Ginny and I have both been busy with—"

"Oh, bosh," Hazel cut in. "Admit it. You're still man-spooked by that experience with Doug."

"Maybe," Constance admitted reluctantly.

"Sweet love, you can't make an omelette without breaking eggs. Why don't *you* call Paul?"

"Paul's a nice guy and all that. But frankly, he just doesn't do it for me."

"'Do it?' You mean he's not quite as sexy and exciting as, say, Quinn Loudon?"

"Hazel! You of all people should know I have no interest in being a gangster's moll."

"Would there be interest if Loudon wasn't a gang-ster?"

"That's sort of like asking what happened before once upon a time. Who knows?"

Her companion met that evasive comment with a mysterious little smile.

By now they had entered the scalloped foothills, and Hazel fell silent, enjoying the sun-luscious day and the magnificent view. The temperature dropped somewhat as they climbed higher, but nothing dramatic.

At one point near the end of the winding ascent up Old Mill Road, they rounded a tight bend and glimpsed a gorge below with white water frothing down it. Both women were almost reluctant when the road finally dead-ended at the Hupenbecker cabin.

"Just like I thought," Constance said, nodding toward the cabin. "Front door standing wide open and the lock broken. Good thing I brought another."

Before they went inside, the two friends walked around back so Hazel could visit the creek and the old stone bridge. It had rained earlier, up here in the mountains, and mud daubers were still active in the puddles.

"They towed Loudon's car out, I see," Constance pointed out. "My God, the tow truck completely tore up the ground."

But the nastiest surprise was reserved for when the two women poked their heads inside the cabin. The place had been so thoroughly "searched" it was actually damaged. Several floorboards had been pried up and carelessly tossed aside.

"Those idiotic goons," Constance fumed. "I'll be sending them a bill. That is, if I can figure out whom to send it to."

Hazel's reaction was more speculative than angry.

"In my long experience with the state troopers and county cops," she told Constance, "they've been quite professional and do everything according to Hoyle. This wasn't their work.''

"Probably federal agents," Constance suggested. "I assume that's who was following me, too. The guy with Ulrick was FBI.''

"Maybe. Did you ask to see any IDs?''

A doubt had seeped into Hazel's tone. Constance glanced at her, startled. "Actually, no. That was dumb, wasn't it? But who else would it be?''

Hazel tossed her own words right back at her. "What happened before once upon a time? It sure looks to me like somebody is mighty danged eager to find Quinn Loudon. Or something they think Loudon has or had.''

Those words made Constance recall how Roger Ulrick had placed such great emphasis on finding out if Loudon gave her anything. She wondered if it was that "ace in the hole" Loudon mentioned. The same thing they were searching for under those torn-up floorboards....

Lost in a complicated labyrinth of inner questions, Constance placed the new padlock in the hasp and secured the cabin.

Everybody talks about the weather, Hazel told herself, but nobody does anything about it.

Well, she was a McCallum, and the McCallums were doers, not talkers.

They were ten miles down the road while everybody else was taking a vote on when to leave. And McCallums never let themselves be daunted by the size of the task at hand.

She had no desire to change the weather—it suited her just fine, especially right now. But as to her beloved town of Mystery, that was a different matter altogether.

She glanced over at Connie's pensive, pretty face as they drove back down to the valley. She admitted to herself that *this* young filly was a real challenge. However, Hazel thrived on challenges; indeed, they were the savory sauce at the banquet of life. The meal would be bland without them.

Hazel had a plan. Her fires were banked, but not her ambition. She wanted, more than anything else, to see Mystery go on being the kind of town it was always meant to be.

But she had to face some hard facts. She was the last McCallum, and she would leave no line behind her. Only one thing could keep Mystery from obliteration under an influx of outsiders and greedy developers: New blood that must be carefully mixed with old. She meant to create new families from the old ones already committed to the town.

She had composed a mental list of good folks in Mystery who needed hitching up. Rodeo champ A.J. Clayburn had been first on that list, and now he was happily married—even a proud new papa. Second on the list was this troubled beauty now driving them down the mountain.

She fiercely admired Constance. That gal lived up to her name: steady and faithful. Rather than flounder from notion to notion, as so many of the younger generation did these days, she had set her sights early on becoming a successful real-estate mandarin. And she'd done it.

The big problem right now, Hazel admitted, was finding just the right man for her.

Doug Huntington had been an outright disaster.

And local fellows like Paul Robeck, "nice guys" and all, just couldn't stir Connie's feminine passions. The man who finally reined in *this* little filly would have to be an outsider. An exceptional one, at that.

But Hazel trusted in serendipity. Her Prussian blue gaze turned to the granite-peaked mountains surrounding them.

She recalled the special tone in Connie's voice every time she mentioned Quinn Loudon, and Hazel's sly little smile was back.

Chapter 6

Quinn Loudon was on her mind when Constance went to bed on Saturday night; he was still there, like a tune she couldn't shake, when she woke up early on Sunday morning. He never really left her thoughts all through the nearly sleepless night.

Exactly why, she couldn't say. Obviously her ordeal had been frightening, but it wasn't just fear she felt. Not for herself, anyway. Something about Loudon, or his plight, made her fear for him.

She had nothing but his word that he was being framed—that, and something she'd never really believed in: so-called "women's intuition." Where was it when she fell for Doug Huntington's phony lines? Nonetheless, she felt it now. Either it was real, or she had been duped yet again by a convincing criminal.

For two nights in a row she had slept poorly, and it required a cold shower and plenty of black coffee to get herself kick-started and chase the cobwebs from her mind. Often she met her family at church on Sunday, then went home with them afterward for breakfast. But this morning she made a beeline to the TV set. The station in Helena featured an "Early Bird Advisory" at seven and eight o'clock, state news, local weather, and sports.

Remote in hand, she plumped down on a corner sofa cluttered with throw pillows her mother had made for her, thick with satin stitch and French knots. She wondered if the Loudon story would lead the news again. Instead, the newscaster—an info-babe with sculpted blond hair—droned on and on about a spectacular twenty-two car pile-up on the interstate near Ironwood.

Constance tuned out the quick-paced images of twisted metal and overturned vehicles. Impatience made her antsy, so she immediately stood up again and began watering her plants, one eye on the TV screen.

Her home was a tidy little two-bedroom of vine-covered brick, nothing elegant but comfortable and efficient. It was actually the yard sprawling all around it that had sold her on the place—a yard that was also home to the most magnificent white-birch trees in Mystery Valley. She had plenty of privacy, her nearest neighbor a quarter-mile away. Yet downtown Mystery was only a ten-minute drive.

She was tilting the water can over a Boston fern in a macramé hanger when the newscaster's voice suddenly riveted her attention.

"—latest on the widening manhunt for Quinn Loudon, the Assistant U.S. Attorney who escaped from authorities in Kalispell on Friday in a hail of bullets."

A picture of Loudon filled the screen for a few

seconds. Constance watched, nervously chewing on her lower lip, while the story cut to a press-conference segment filmed late yesterday. A federal prosecutor identified as Dolph Merriday, the same spokesman she recalled from the radio report on Friday, was speaking into a clutter of microphones. The podium featured the seal of the U.S. Justice Department.

"We now have ample evidence that Loudon is an incorrigible criminal. Even as I speak, this fugitive's probably out robbing poorboxes somewhere to finance his getaway."

"But Mr. Merriday," a reporter spoke up, "today I interviewed Quinn Loudon's legal counsel, Lance Pollard. What about Loudon's claim that Sheriff Cody Anders's unexplained disappearance is linked to the investigation, and that he and Loudon overheard a bribe between two key legal players in Montana road construction?"

Constance frowned at the sarcastic twist of Merriday's mouth.

"Yes," he replied, "I've heard that claim, too. Perhaps this supposed 'bribe' was in fact what the paranormal experts call a clairvoyant experience?" he suggested with obvious scorn. "Or far more likely, it's an obvious and pathetic attempt to point the finger of blame elsewhere."

The prosecutor wore a blue suit, no doubt chosen, she told herself, to accent his silver hair and project an aura of unassailable authority. And no doubt he'd succeeded.

But something about Merriday's remarks—on TV and radio—niggled at her. She couldn't understand this great effort to spin the story so it always emphasized Quinn Loudon's supposed criminal nature, rather than his alleged crimes. She realized, of course, that all lawyers attacked the moral character of their adversaries. But they did it in the courtroom, usually, not over the airwaves.

It was almost as if they wanted to convict him through the media as soon as possible. Perhaps, an inner voice suggested, that makes it much easier to quell the concern if Quinn Loudon doesn't turn up alive. Just one more hardened criminal who "got his."

The info-babe donned a playful smile and bounced to a fluff piece about a hot-dog eating contest in Billings. Constance turned off the TV set. She admonished herself against drawing unwarranted conclusions about Quinn Loudon's innocence.

She tried to work in the office she'd set up in the spare bedroom. Most pressing was a sheaf of legal forms she needed to fill out for a sale she had closed last week on a nice little A-frame cottage in the south valley. But she simply couldn't concentrate, right now, on the legal niceties of escrow accounts and variable mortgage rates.

She decided to run some errands in town. She'd been so busy with this year's surprise influx of home buyers—not to mention surprise abductions at gunpoint—that almost everything in her refrigerator was near or past the sell-by date. Since the pharmacy was open on Sunday, she decided she should also renew the prescription for her allergy medicine.

She had parked the rental car on the concrete apron in front of her attached garage. As she eased down the serpentine driveway, she searched everywhere for any sign of the gray sedan that had followed her—or so she still believed—yesterday.

However, the only vehicle she spotted on the road to town was Billy Bettinger's old rattletrap pickup and drilling rig. Billy had dug water wells throughout the valley ever since she could remember. She waved as he flashed past her, and he honked back.

Seeing Billy coaxed the day's first smile onto her lips. The shameless but harmless old lech never saw her without letting loose a sharp wolf whistle.

"Prettiest gal in the valley," he always insisted. "All them curves, and me with no brakes."

"Big talk," she had shot back once in a challenging tone, and Billy had blushed to the tips of his sunburned ears.

Thanks in part to the unseasonably warm weather, Mystery was already fairly busy when she angle-parked in front of Omensetter's Pharmacy on Main Street. Newcomers and longtime residents mingled on the sidewalks and frequented the various shops and the brand-new supermarket.

She quickly realized, from Wallace Omensetter's remarks as he filled her prescription, that the brief link to Mystery had gotten the Quinn Loudon story noised about all over the valley.

"Saw your sign on the news, Connie," he informed her. "Got yourself a free plug on TV, huh?"

"My sign?" she repeated, confused at first.

Wallace wore a longhorn mustache, the kind she saw only in cornball TV commercials featuring "Old West" characters.

"Sure. Yesterday, or actually last night on the late news. They showed the cabin where that fellow Jim Loudon holed up. I recognized the Hupenbecker place right off."

"Quinn," she corrected him automatically. She must have gone to bed before that broadcast.

As Wallace handed her the medicine, he bent close to her over the counter, his lopsided mouth grimly self-important under the silly mustache.

"Around here," he said in a confidential hush, though the store was empty except for them, "rumors are always thicker 'n toads after a hard rain. But I heard this straight from Constable Lofton. This guy Loudon? He's a notorious bank robber. You watch yourself. Lofton thinks he might even have infiltrated the town in disguise."

Her skeptical dimple appeared for a moment. But she gave him a solemn nod, trying to keep a straight face. She wasn't sure exactly what "notorious bank robbers" looked like these days. But she suspected that one would stand out in this valley populated by ranchers, townies, and diva-shaded yuppies like a rhinestone yo-yo.

"Thanks for the tip," she replied from a poker face. "I'll be careful."

But as she left the pharmacy, Constance felt a stab of guilt. There had been several messages on her answering machine that she hadn't bothered answering yet. Now she realized that at least one of them might have been her mom, worried by that graphic of the cabin and her real-estate sign.

She decided to stop by her parents' place before she went shopping at the supermarket. Five minutes later, she parked alongside the curb in front of their big white frame house on Silver Street.

The moment she opened the kitchen door, she realized she had guessed right. Dorothy Adams turned from the stove and sent her oldest child a familiar glance that mixed one part relief with two parts reproof.

"Constance Adams, if you weren't so big I'd fan your britches right now! What's the big idea of not returning my calls?"

Calls. Plural. She felt more guilt lance through her. Constance crossed the big, cheery room and gave her mom a hug, feeling kitchen-warmed skin through her mother's print dress.

"Beth Ann called last night, and I told her I was okay," she replied. "Didn't she tell you?"

"She grunted something about you still being alive, yes. But I wanted to talk to you myself."

Constance watched her mother drop homemade dumplings into a pot of simmering chicken broth. "Your dad's still at church," she added. "He's refereeing the dartball tournament against Mount Zion."

Seven-year-old Mickey, the youngest, ran into the kitchen making fire-truck noises. He circled his big sister twice, then abruptly halted with an ear-piercing squeal meant to sound like brakes.

"Lookit my new shirt, Connie! Aunt Janet gived it to me."

"Gave, honey, not gived." Constance read the T-shirt message out loud: "Bee it ever so bumble, there's no place like comb."

She laughed. "That's cute, sweetie."

"*Girls* are sweeties," he corrected her. "I'm a fireman!"

Mickey zoomed off to put out fires elsewhere in the house. Constance could hear Beth Ann and Pattie bickering in the next room. Beth Ann poked her head into the kitchen just long enough to taunt smugly,

"See, Connie? Didn't I tell you? 'Beware the eighth house!'"

She was gone again before Constance could answer.

"It *does* give the heart a jupe," her mom agreed, turning from the stove and wiping her hands on her apron. "My goodness, Connie, what if you and your client had been up there when that...that man was there?"

Constance had debated telling her mother more about what happened. However, the worry in her eyes scotched that idea.

But something else occurred to her. Beth Ann, too, must have assumed the client was not Quinn Loudon. She had no reason to assume otherwise.

Why had she, Constance, been left out of the details relayed to the media? After all, she gave the Montana State Troopers a complete account of events.

She was grateful, of course, to have been spared the unwanted publicity. But it hardly seemed likely anyone would have deliberately spared her for benevolent reasons.

Unless, that inner voice whispered, somebody doesn't want any attention on you. Because public attention is, after all, a form of protection....

She lost the thought as the argument between Beth Ann and Pattie escalated in volume.

"Spackoid!"

"Gumbah!"

"Zorch!"

"Boffo!"

"You two knock it off in there!" Dorothy called out. She sent Constance a puzzle-headed glance. "Did you understand *any* of that?"

Constance rolled her eyes. "Boffo vaguely rings a bell. I think it's theater slang. But don't ask me, I grew up in the geeks-and-nerds generation."

"Neither one of those girls," Dorothy lamented, "can get a decent grade in a foreign-language class. But they sure sound fluent in *some*thing besides English."

"I just stopped to see if you need anything from the supermarket."

Dorothy shook her head. She had never quite accepted the notion of such a huge store within the town limits. "I just went yesterday. Their meat is cheap, but none of these chain places has ever heard of a decent tomato. It's all this genetically engineered stuff now. Thanks for asking though, hon."

Constance was heading out the door when her mother called behind her. "Connie? You be careful, hear? That Quinn Loudon is still on the loose."

"Oh, don't worry so much," her daughter assured her. "The whole thing's a weekend wonder, that's all. It'll blow over soon."

Despite her earlier worrying, Constance began to take heart at her own words. She probably *was* just being paranoid. It was only natural, of course, to be concerned about Quinn Loudon and even to wonder if he was being set up as he claimed. But her role in his drama was behind her. It was ridiculous to assume *she* was somehow involved any further.

Constance eased the white Taurus away from the curb and headed across town toward the supermarket on the eastern outskirts of Mystery. The day was still young. She resolved to get her shopping done, then go home and log onto the computer. She and Ginny were in the process of designing a Web site for Mystery Valley Real Estate.

She eased over the railroad hump near the end of the street and signaled for a right turn onto Main. Her eyes cut to the rearview mirror, and in seconds her palms were sweaty.

A gray sedan was behind her, right turn signal slyly winking at her.

Without really planning to, Constance accelerated right on past the supermarket and bore due east toward the mountains.

The gray car followed her with the persistence of a jet contrail. No wondering about it now, she realized. There was definitely someone following her.

As it did yesterday, the car never pulled close enough so she could distinguish a face. She was sure, though, that it was only one occupant in the vehicle, the driver. She couldn't be sure whether male or female.

She fought to keep her breathing even. The parking lots and buildings quickly dwindled away to fallow, winter-brown pastures and wheat fields on both sides. Dead ahead, the mountains rose precipitously, their uppermost gullies white with wind-packed snow.

Don't panic, she rallied herself. That's the main thing, just keeping a cool head. Whoever this was must have deliberately eased off yesterday. Probably to put her off-guard.

Hazel's comment was still fresh in memory. *Those feds are a fox-eared tribe, all right.*

They're toying with me, Constance told herself. Trying to unnerve me. Heaven knows why....

But other comments, less welcome than Hazel's,

were also fresh in memory. Including Roger Ulrick's accusation yesterday about Quinn Loudon: *You seem worried about his well-being.* Perhaps they had decided that any signs of sympathy made her a "collaborator."

She had to consider another angle, one even more frightening. If Quinn Loudon had told the truth, there was at least a fifty-fifty chance the person following her—agent or not—was not carrying out legitimate orders in the pursuit of justice. But rather, to pursue the *obstruction* of justice. Whatever that required...

By now this person knew where she lived, of course. So throwing him off her tail was, at best, a purely symbolic gesture. In fact, the effort to do so only increased her own apparent guilt.

But the threatening tactics being used against her made Constance instinctively want to fight back. It was highly unlikely this person behind her knew the back roads and remote trails up in the mountains. She had done plenty of mountain-bike riding up there when she was younger. She knew the slopes as well as any Mystery native—which roads were blocked by wash-outs, which narrow fire lanes could be driven by car and which would bog a vehicle up to its axles in mud.

She felt her nervous stomach settle as determination and the lure of competition replaced her fear.

"Let's go for a little ride, my impolite friend," she muttered, toeing the accelerator.

In his feverish and delirious dreams, Quinn Loudon moved through successive patches of fog. As each dense fog thinned to harsh, burning sunlight, singsong voices rose, taunting him.

Children's voices, reverberating off the brick walls
surrounding a school yard:

Quinn! Quinn!
He's our man!
His ma 'n' pa
Are in the slam!

But sometimes, when the roiling fog cleared, the
taunting children were gone. Instead, Jim and Ceil
Westphal would be waiting for him to appear, love in
their eyes. Jim tall and broad-shouldered and proud
in his best dress uniform, badge flashing in the sunlight like diamond dust.

Then the fog would close in on him again, cloying
and dense, clammy fog enveloping him....

Loudon lay semiconscious, his jacket folded under
his head. He shivered violently, for it was colder up
here. Inside his feverish head, the taunting voices rose
again like the harsh squawking of crows.

Quinn! Quinn!
He's our man!
His ma 'n' pa
Are in the slam!

Constance put the rental car through its pacings and
then some. She had expected a real all-terrain chase.
But her pursuer ended up skidding into an erosion
gully on the very first shale-littered slope.

She left him there, spinning his rear wheels and
digging himself in deeper. Her first ebullient rush of

elation, however, gave way quickly to the gnawing question of Quinn Loudon and his whereabouts.

Constance followed a narrow fire lane until it debouched onto Old Mill Road. A right turn would take her back down into the valley and the safety of witnesses; a left turn, and she'd dead-end at the Hupenbecker cabin.

She turned left, telling herself this hunch she felt was completely irrational. Even if Loudon had returned, out of sheer desperation, to the cabin, he'd be out of luck. The place was locked up tight again.

The car twisted through the last crinkum-crankum turn, and the cabin suddenly lunged into view. She could see in a glance that all was well—no vehicles, and the shiny new padlock still secured the heavy slab door.

No need to even get out of the car. She was starting to back out when she abruptly pressed the brake pedal, then slid the gearshift into park.

When she turned off the ignition, there was suddenly only the silence broken by insect rhythms.

Might as well check out back, too, she decided. Just a quick peek, she added as she stepped out of the car. The car door made a hollow *chunk* sound that echoed down the slope.

It was the red, mud-splattered rear fender of the Jeep she spotted first when she reached a rear corner of the cabin. That was startling enough and made her heart begin to race.

But that same heart lurched hard, and she cried out when she spotted Quinn Loudon—or rather, his body—sprawled in the front seat.

However, he wasn't dead yet. Her brief cry had

roused his eyelids halfway open. He lifted his head just long enough to recognize who had made it.

His handsome upper lip somehow stretched into a little ironic smile of welcome.

"A bad penny always turns up, huh?" he greeted her in a faltering voice.

Before she could even trust her own voice to answer, his smoky gray eyes lost their focus and he slumped unconscious.

Chapter 7

"Mr. Loudon? Mr. Loudon, can you hear me?"

Evidently he could, but all he could manage was an exhausted groan in response, then a slight nod of confirmation. He was shivering violently, his lips chapped and swollen, so dry and cracked they were bleeding; his complexion was ashen gray, and though his wound wasn't doing any fresh bleeding, dried blood splotched his pants leg like a rust stain.

Constance lay the back of one hand against his feverish, beard-shadowed cheek. His breathing was still strong, but ragged and uneven.

"You are a bad penny," she told him in helpless frustration. But she noticed, too, how long she hesitated to pull her hand away from his cheek. The humid warmth of his breath on her fingers made a soft, responsive warmth stir inside her.

One part of her, the logical part, voted to turn him over to the authorities right now. After all, she had no right to second-guess the law no matter how oddly some of its minions behaved.

But as she watched his chest rise and fall, and studied the planes and angles of his handsome face, her heart pleaded with her head to hide him. Somebody meant to kill him, not simply arrest him. That gray car she'd just eluded back on the mountain slopes lent credence to his story. So did the lack of mention of the missing sheriff. She'd yet to hear what was behind the strange disappearance of Cody Anders.

"Mr. Loudon? Can you hear me?"

"Hear me," he repeated, not quite coming round.

She fought to remain calm while she tried to think. *The gun.* She had to get that from him while she could. Then somehow she had to get him out of this cold.

She reached inside his jacket and felt the soft chamois holster. Her fingers closed round the checkered rubber grip of the weapon. Careful, she cautioned herself, keep the muzzle pointed away—

It was halfway out of the holster when his voice startled her.

"Won't do either of us…any good," he muttered as if half in, half out of a coma. But his eyes were open and looking up at her. "No bullets left."

"You certainly had bullets on Friday," she reminded him. "At the courthouse in Kalispell."

"'At the courthouse' is right. I deliberately put those two slugs high in the wall, a yard over the marshals' heads."

His eyes closed for a few seconds, then opened slowly. "Anyway, it was the last two shells I had," he assured her. "It's been empty ever since."

Her first blush of anger at herself, for being so gullible, passed quickly. What did it matter, she thought. I would have driven him anyway—he'd been intimidating enough without the gun. She was convinced he really would have steered them into a ditch if she hadn't cooperated.

Something still held her back now, too. It would be only a few moments' effort to dig out her phone and call 911. No gun threatening her this time, and obviously Quinn Loudon was too weak to manhandle a kitten. So why did he still have this hold over her?

"Mr. Loudon, you *must* get to a doctor. You—"

"No doctor," he insisted. He tried to rise up on one elbow but gave up and slumped to the dashboard again. "Doctor'll…turn me in…they'll kill me."

"Who? Who will kill you?"

But he was out of it again, skating along the borderline of awareness, groaning something incoherent. She realized she had to do something or he'd possibly die from exposure while she dithered.

She glanced at the Jeep. It was a sheet of mud from front fenders to rear, and broken-off bushes were wedged under the bumpers. The passenger-side mirror had been bent, too. But she spotted no serious damage. Evidently Loudon had resorted to four-wheel drive and left the roads completely at some point, no doubt to elude pursuers.

She doubted very much that he could have made it into Billings and back. Not with every cop in the state on the lookout for him.

Her mind worked quickly, settling on the least problematic plan of action. If she took her Jeep, and left the rental car here, that left her with the problem of explaining to the law just how she got her Jeep back from him. It also left the thorny problem of who would bring her back up here to get the rental car.

For a moment she was tempted to call Hazel—the one person she knew who would keep a cool head and give sound advice. But another, more chilling thought occurred to her. Hazel's power extended only so far—even she might be in harm's way if dragged into this.

"No way around it," she decided out loud. "I'm on my own."

Her immediate course of action was now clear. Loudon's deteriorating condition was first priority. She'd simply leave the Jeep where it was and let the authorities find it. That way there was no proof she had crossed paths again with Quinn Loudon.

She hurried around front, started the Taurus, and backed it around the corner of the cabin. She parked as close to Loudon as she could, then opened a back door of the car.

"Mr. Loudon? Can you hear me? Mr. Loudon!"

"Mr. Loudon," he repeated in a whisper. "Hear me…"

"Mr. Loudon, *please* wake up. Wake up and help me."

She never could have lifted him into the car by herself. He was well over six feet and powerfully built. But Loudon possessed just enough remaining strength to work with her when she tugged him up into a sitting position, then wrestled his bulk into the back seat of the car.

Exhaustion and loss of blood, aggravated by the colder air up here, had left him giddy, even silly.

"Bad girl," he chastized her as she struggled to stuff his long legs into the car. "Naughty lady with amber eyes. Helps criminal Quinn…there goes *her* spot in heaven…"

"If I were you," she warned the semiconscious man, "I'd choose a different theme for my babbling. You're pushing your luck."

"Push my luck," he repeated. "Quinn, Quinn, he's our man…."

She got in behind the wheel and turned the heater on. Ignoring the deliriously rambling man in the backseat, she wheeled onto Old Mill Road and headed back down the mountain. With each bend in the road, she expected to spot the gray sedan.

She fought to control her inner turmoil. No matter what her instincts told her about this stranger, she was still a criminal in the eyes of everyone else if she got caught helping him. Which naturally made her wonder how she could be doing something like this after the shame and humiliation Doug Huntington put her through.

True, most folks in Mystery had been too kind to openly pity her. But she'd felt it behind their greetings and small talk: *Poor girl, practically jilted at the altar.* Even though she was the one who called off the wedding, not Doug. Such events never got recorded accurately in township lore. Rather, they became what Hazel sneered at as "saloon gossip."

But even saloon gossip, Constance realized, couldn't exaggerate the mess she was in now.

The car shimmied hard as it rolled over a stretch of washboard road. Loudon muttered behind her, "His ma 'n' pa are in the slam."

Against all her expectations, Constance made it home without incident. Now she faced the problem of where to put her abductor-turned-patient.

As the car nosed into the long driveway, she pressed her garage-door opener. Despite the clutter of bicycles, lawn mower, storm windows, and extra FOR SALE signs stored inside the attached garage, she was able to shoehorn the Taurus inside and just barely close the door behind her.

"Mr. Loudon? Can you hear me?" she asked as she opened the back door of the car. A single, un-shaded, 25-watt bulb hanging from a long string was the only illumination.

"Hear you, Mr. Loudon," he repeated. "Thirsty…Mr. Loudon thirsty, hear you?"

Once again he helped her just enough that she was able to get him out of the car. But he immediately slumped in her arms, his knees simply unhinging.

She knew she could never get him into the house while he was like this.

With his head and shoulders propped against her legs, she cast a quick glance around the cluttered garage. There was her old futon rolled up against the big box of Christmas-tree ornaments. She could leave him right there, she decided. At least for now, with plenty of blankets. Nobody ever came into the garage, anyway. It was the safest place in the house. But there was no heat, so if the temperature took a nose dive, he'd have to come inside.

She let him slide gently down to the floor, then moved her mountain bike and some other things, quickly clearing a little area to unroll the futon. When she had him resting comfortably on it, she opened the garage door and backed the rental car out onto the concrete parking apron. She came back inside and shut the overhead door again with the automatic opener.

The only other door in the garage led into the kitchen, so she was able to quickly assemble some necessary items without opening the garage door again. Loudon was conscious the next time she bent over him. His variable eyes were almost teal in the dim light of the single overhead bulb.

"These should help with the fever and pain," she told him, shaking two extra-strength caplets into her hand. Her other hand supported the back of his head while he drank from the glass of water she held to his lips.

He almost coughed up the caplets, but drank greedily. He even tried to tip the glass more when she stopped, but Constance kept pulling it back to slow him down so he wouldn't choke.

"Well, Miss Adams," he said in a weak but clear voice. "Looks like you've gone way beyond rendering good-Samaritan aid."

"I don't need a smirking lawyer to tell me that," she assured him as she wiped a damp sponge over his face.

"Who's smirking? I don't feel *that* good."

"It's in your voice, not your face."

He raised his bemused face enough to glance at her hands, busy at the front of his trousers.

"You say such things to me while you undo my belt? I'm receiving a mixed signal here," he muttered weakly.

"I hate to rain all over your parade, but you're not getting any signals whatsoever," she assured him. "Either I ruin your trousers with the scissors, or I take them down. I have to look at your wound."

Her practical, lecturing tone coaxed a smile onto his tired face.

"Look at my...wound," he repeated, pausing suggestively and letting his tone tease her. "Promise not to peek anywhere else? I'm very bashful."

"I'll try very, very hard to control myself," she assured him. "Now lift up your hips, I can't...there."

His trousers slid down, bunching around his muscular thighs. She was grateful for the long tails on his dress shirt. They made it easier to maintain some modesty.

"Roll over on your stomach," she told him.

He complied, wincing at the effort.

Pressing her bottom lip between her teeth, she forced herself to study the angry, blue-black, puckered flesh where the bullet had entered the muscle of his thigh in back.

She bathed the area in hydrogen peroxide, then soaped it clean.

"It looks like maybe you got lucky," she pronounced after a minute of close scrutiny. "I think the bullet went in at an angle and came out near the front.

"Yes," she confirmed a second later, studying the muscular bulge of thigh muscle on the front of his leg. There was another wound there. An exit wound. She also held up the expensive fabric of his trousers. "Here's a second small tear where the bullet must've come out."

He seemed to ignore all this. Staring at her with those unsettling smoky eyes, he finally asked, "Why are you helping me?" A long pause ensued. "You know you're harboring a fugitive."

"Maybe I'm just a dumb female who hasn't got a

clue. Or maybe I just like to live dangerously, Mr. Loudon. You know—another wholesome, hometown girl who secretly craves life on the edge with a bad boy.''

He mustered enough energy to give a little snort. ''I'd say something sarcastic, but your ironic tone beat me to it.''

''By now,'' she told him as she poured another glass of water from a plastic pitcher, ''infection from your wound may have spread to your bloodstream. That might explain your fever. If you're not allergic to penicillin, take these antibiotics. I'll give you two now and another two every few hours.''

''Yes, Doctor,'' he quipped. ''Or is it R.N.?''

''My aunt Janet's the nurse. These are left over from a strep infection last month.''

He swallowed two along with the entire glass of water.

''What day is this?'' he asked suddenly as he handed the glass back to her. Their hands brushed as she took it, and both of them seemed momentarily startled.

''Sunday,'' she told him. ''It's about 2:00 p.m.''

''You have got to be kidding.'' He groaned as he collapsed back onto the futon. ''I don't *believe* I wasted more than an entire day driving out in the boonies. Driving in circles, at that.''

''Why did you come back to the cabin?''

He ran his hand over his face as if in exasperation. ''I figured after I dropped you that you'd tell the authorities I was headed for Billings. That was the last place I wanted to go until the heat wore off. So I came back to Mystery. With no place to go or hide,

I found my way back to the cabin. It was my only salvation.''

"Roll over again," she ordered. "I need to put a dressing on your wound."

This time she had to help him. While she wrapped and taped the wound, he explained his aborted trip to Billings.

"You must have called in the cavalry on me right away," he lamented.

"Excuse me, I was still a law-abiding citizen then. Hold *still*," she added.

"They had a checkpoint set up before I got twenty miles. I shifted your Jeep into four-wheel and hit the slopes. Man, that thing walks up walls, doesn't it?"

"I guess it does, now. *Please* stop wiggling, I can't—"

"Well dammit, it hurts! Anyhow, I didn't drive the whole time. I was too tired. I hid and slept for most of it. I followed whatever fire trails I could find, hit a couple dirt roads. God knows how I made it back to the cabin."

"God knows," she repeated ironically. "Just awful blessed, I guess. There, it's bandaged. I put ointment on the dressing so it won't stick. You can pull your trousers up now."

"Thanks. You're a good nurse—nice hands," he observed as he wiggled his pants over his hips.

"I shall treasure that compliment in the locket of my heart." Her tone altered, became more serious as she added, "To whom shall I send the bill—Roger Ulrick or Todd Mumford?"

His eyelids had begun to ease shut. Now they snapped wide open. He even tried to sit up, but abandoned the effort.

"You spoke with them?" he demanded.

"Spoke? It wasn't exactly a coffeeklatch. They woke me up on Saturday morning in my motel room."

She knew that even if she was wrong about Loudon, even if he was guilty, it wouldn't matter if she told him what the D.A. and the FBI agent had asked her. He listened carefully, especially when she mentioned Ulrick's emphasis on what it was that Loudon needed to get in Billings.

"Since those two interrogated me," she concluded, "someone has been following me. Someone in a gray sedan. I gave him the slip today just before I found you. Whoever it is could be watching my house right now."

He remained silent for some time after she quit speaking, letting all this soak in, his handsome, beard-scruffed features set rigid as granite.

"Mumford," he finally told her, "is on the up-and-up. Straight-arrow and by the book. The quiet type who sees more than most people realize. I'll vouch for him. But Ulrick?"

He paused, his cracked lips twitching into a parody of a grin. "Hearing he's in the mix worries me. He's way over his head in debt. First he took a tough hit on the foreign stock markets. Then he went through a messy divorce that's still being litigated. He's got some serious debt issues, or that's the buzz around the office water cooler, anyway."

"Serious debts? You mean, serious enough that he could be involved in these kickbacks you've been investigating?"

Loudon nodded. "Sure. He was on my list to check

out—the list they claim I compiled as bribery targets.''

''The news hasn't mentioned that, I don't think.''

''TV keeps it simple. But I knew it had to go further than just Jeremy Schrader and Brandon Whitaker. I can see Ulrick getting hungry for a little percentage, then, when the scam goes public, taking...extraordinary steps to cover up his dirt.''

''What would be 'extraordinary steps'?'' she asked.

He stared at her. His only words were, ''Cody Anders would know.''

Quinn fell back against the futon while Constance left for the kitchen with the used gauze and cotton. A few moments later he began thinking. None of it settled well with him.

They would toss his apartment in Billings. And his office. That was all right, let them. They wouldn't find it. He learned from the best. Always hide your hole card.

After all, his evidence boiled down to one computer disk full of geometric accusations and statistical innuendos. The mathematical equivalent, in law enforcement, of genetic match-ups. Probability science applied to routine phone and financial records to establish a pattern of money-laundering by Schrader and Whitaker—and others, if only he could have found time to prove it. Others like Ulrick and perhaps even Dolph Merriday.

He just hoped his evidence wasn't too high-tech and ''academic'' for the court system. It lacked the drama of a tearful confession or a crime caught on video.

But once it sank in, it would surely shift the prosecutor's focus away from him and onto them. With luck, the courts would use his data to subpoena a few key records. That additional data, in turn, could provide scientifically impressive evidence to trump their hearsay and planted evidence against him.

He started, realizing she'd returned from the kitchen. Now she stared down at him with those witchy amber eyes this time filled with inquiry, not hostility.

"What the hell am I doing?" she whispered as if for her ears alone.

"It's dangerous enough that you're helping me. But it's absolutely reckless for me to be telling you what it is they want. I've already said too much."

"*Now* you're stricken with conscience?" The warmth of indignation rose in her cheeks. "You tell a lie to lure me into the mountains. You pull a gun out on me—"

"I object. I *showed* you the gun," he corrected her. "It was never 'on' you. Technically, you know, it's called 'brandishing' a weapon as opposed to a direct threat of force."

"Listen to the lawyer crank it up," she mocked him, gathering her medical and cleaning supplies. "No doubt you could lay a feather on a rock and prove it's a sofa, too. But *I* won't sleep on it. You know, you also stole my Jeep. And now, all of a sudden, you're afraid to get 'reckless' with me? Don't insult my intelligence, Mr. Quinn. I liked you better when you were simply an honest ruffian."

"If you really feel that way," he replied quietly, avoiding her angry eyes, "then why not just turn me in? There's no gun *on* you now, is there?"

"Maybe I will," she fired back over her shoulder as she headed toward the kitchen door.

"Go ahead. I'm damned if I'm begging your pity. Tell them I forced you again. Say I raped you, I won't deny it. You'll get out of this clean. If you're awfully lucky, that is."

She turned, one hand on the doorknob. "What do you mean, if I'm lucky?"

He was clearly tiring again, and it cost him an obvious effort to be heard across the width of the garage.

"I mean that, like it or not, it appears Ulrick either doesn't believe, or is at least suspicious of, the answers you gave him in your motel room."

"Maybe he's given up on me," she pointed out. "Nobody's been here or even called."

"Maybe, maybe not. Even if they do manage to kill me before I can sing, will someone start worrying about *you?* You met Ulrick—I'm telling you that guy's a nutcase. Being prosecutor types, these guys are good at covering their butts. It wouldn't take much, in rugged country like this, to have a terrible 'accident' while driving a steep mountain road."

Her expression froze, as if a chill slid down the bumps of her spine.

"You're just saying that so I won't turn you in," she accused.

"Baloney, and you know it. This whole situation has gone way beyond the usual paint-by-numbers law. I don't mean just your helping me—think about Roger Ulrick's behavior when he interrogated you. Some people think the guy's just a squirrel. I think he's another type of rodent altogether."

She did think about Ulrick, and she had to agree with Quinn's assessment of him. She also thought about her distinct impression regarding Dolph Merriday's radio and TV remarks—how they seemed designed to hang the no-good label on Loudon, emphasizing his supposedly dangerous criminal nature.

"Why don't you get some rest?" she finally said, her tone exasperated. "I'm not turning you in. I'm just going to fix you something to eat. I happen to think you're either telling all the truth or most of it. I...I believe you're the victim here, although your stubborn nature and bluntness have no doubt contributed to your troubles. I wouldn't call you a master of diplomacy."

"Fair enough," he replied, starting to lose the fight to stay alert. "But I mean it when I say you have to quit worrying solely about my motivations. Until this thing changes dramatically, I advise you to consider your own safety first."

It was on her lips to retort: "That's rich, coming from *you*." After all, he was the reason for this horrible mess that had entangled her like a giant net.

Unless he was telling the truth, she reminded herself, as you profess to believe. In which case he was a victim of the crime, not the author of it.

She felt herself relenting a bit, and for just a few moments the humor of her dilemma struck her.

"Do you realize," she asked him, "that I'm in more danger if you're really the decent man I hope you are?"

"Cross your fingers," he barely managed, half asleep already. "Maybe I'll turn out to be a liar yet."

No thank you, she told him silently as she headed inside for more blankets. *I'd prefer the danger to the lies.*

* * *

"Morning, Cas," Hazel greeted her foreman from a cell phone. "Did I wake you up?"

"Would it matter if you did?" grumbled Caswell Snyder. "You caught me in my skivvies, boss, but I'm wide awake."

"I don't wonder," Hazel said, chuckling. "I can hear the bawling over the phone—you've got the yearling heifers separated, haven't you?"

"All ready for the alley," Cas confirmed. "You want to come on up and supervise?"

Hazel considered for a moment. Usually this waited until after the spring melt. But taking advantage of the late-season grass, the herds had been driven to the outlying summer pastures, up on the lower mountain slopes. That way there'd be grass left down in the valley when the cattle returned to the home range.

For the next couple days the yearling heifers would be worked through narrow corrals while expert eyes decided which to keep for breeding and which to sell to the feedlots. Usually she assisted Cas. This amounted to the two of them praising their own picks while insulting—good-naturedly but vigorously—the other guy's obvious bad judgment.

This particular morning, however, Hazel was working on a project even dearer to her than selecting the Lazy M's breedlines. She was helping to form Mystery Valley's, too, or so she hoped.

"You and Charlie take care of it," she decided, meaning the Lazy M's top hand, Charlie Bursons. "Neither one of you tinhorns knows an Aberdeen Angus from a government mule. But I've got mischief closer to home to tend to."

"Good," Cas fired back. "We can cuss and spit better without a woman around."

"Why, Cas, there's cussing every time I come up to line camp."

"Huh. That's just Sunday cussin' you hear. We shame the devil when you ain't around."

"I leave you to your conscience then," Hazel signed off, retracting the phone's short antenna and dropping the unit into the big front pocket of her sweater. She stood in the doorway that led from her kitchen to the side yard and the mostly empty corrals beyond. She had already been wide awake when the birds began celebrating sunup.

At the moment, however, her attention was focused on a radio clock sitting next to the toaster oven on her S-shaped kitchen counter.

"—vehicle Loudon had allegedly stolen was found abandoned at the same remote mountain cabin where he first allegedly commandeered it and the vehicle's owner. Tire tracks indicate he may have been picked up by an accomplice." The newscaster reported smoothly in a pleasant baritone voice. "Authorities report no progress in the search for the fugitive assistant U.S. attorney. However, the search effort has intensified in the mountains surrounding Mystery Valley. According to one federal spokesman, agents equipped with starlight goggles are even scouring the rugged terrain after dark, hoping to locate the fugitive's infrared heat images...."

"That's what you say," Hazel remarked to the unseen newscaster before she moved back inside the house to switch off the radio.

She buttoned her cotton sweater as she went outside into the early-morning chill. The sun was still only a ruddy promise in the east, and nighttime mist lingered over the surrounding pastures. It had gotten cold enough, last night, to lightly frost the grass.

A day so fresh, she told herself, you just wanted to fill your lungs with it over and over, and thank the Creator for the chance.

Nonetheless, her thoughts lingered on the news report she'd just heard. Like anyone else, she knew only what the law and the media mavens let her hear. But she also sensed another slant to this Quinn Loudon story.

Partly that was because of Connie's manner. The handsome fugitive with the football shoulders was sure giving somebody fits... *Tire tracks indicate an accomplice.* The line irked Hazel like an unseen nettle.

The exact part the young Realtor had played in the still unfolding drama was still unknown. But Hazel knew that girl was up to something, all right. Connie had been too quiet lately, for one thing.

And other people were being too quiet about Connie. Deliberately quiet.

Whatever she was up to, it smelled like it involved Quinn Loudon. And it was something to which once-burned, twice-shy Connie was having to respond to with her heart—a dicey proposition, at best.

Hazel knew full well what a risk love could be: an auto accident had killed the only man she ever gave her heart to. It took him away less than a year after their wedding and before their union produced a child.

For her, there had been no option but to honor her vows forever. Her passion had been violent and enduring. Even to this day she could remember how his words were rough and determined when he'd made his proposal: he'd told her she was a McCallum before she married him and she would be one afterward too, and that he didn't want some namby-pamby female hooking her claws into him, taking on his name and not standing on her own. She was strong and independent in her own right, and that's why he loved her, and wanted her to be his wife.

So she, Hazel McCallum, had been forced to become even more strong and independent. Because her only love had died. Because she'd fallen hopelessly and eternally in love with the only man to prove her match.

But for all the grief of that unutterable loss, Hazel still believed that some were meant to take the risk. She suspected Connie was taking it now—or about to, although she might not fully realize that yet.

And perhaps she was doomed to repeat the same mistake she made with Doug.

Some people never learn, bless their oft-broken hearts. But at least Connie was rolling the dice, taking her big chance....

And once in a while, Hazel reminded herself, a gamble pays off big.

She herself was gambling on Mystery, for example, at a time when the ''nattering nabobs of negativism'' swore the little community was doomed to lose its unique frontier character. Doomed to become one more impersonal strip-mall town surrounded by a fast-food jungle.

Hazel's bright, vital eyes rose to the dusky mountain peaks on her right, and she smiled.

No, she had not forgotten the snows of yesteryear—nor the fiery passions, either. But the world belonged to the living, and her eye was fixed firmly on the future.

Mystery, *her* Mystery, not some anonymous developer's, would survive if those who lived here loved this town enough to keep it alive. The way Connie Adams loved it, for one.

Hazel recalled one of her favorite descriptions of God: subtle but not malicious.

She thought—with all due humility, of course— how that same description applied rather nicely to her, too.

Unfortunately, her heart told her Connie faced a dilemma that subtlety alone would not resolve. She sensed it—that girl's mettle was about to be tested, and tested hard.

Chapter 8

Despite brief rallying periods, Quinn Loudon battled his fever throughout the long night. Tormented by guilt for not calling a doctor, Constance threw on some warm clothing and hovered over the sick man for most of the night. Exhaustion finally claimed her around 2:00 a.m., and she fell into her bed moments after undressing.

She woke at the first rays of sunlight slanting through the bedroom window. Seven o'clock, according to the alarm clock on her nightstand. For a few blessed moments she automatically geared up for her Monday morning back-to-the-office routine.

Then, in a rush of troubling memories and images, she remembered the fugitive hidden in her garage.

"Quinn Loudon," she said out loud to the silent bedroom. She switched on the radio on her nightstand, but she'd just missed the state news.

She wrapped a terry-cloth robe around herself and stepped into a pair of flat-heeled slippers.

He might have taken a turn for the worse while she slept, she reminded herself. Or maybe he'd done something *el flippo* again, like steal the rental car.

As she hurried through the silent hallway, she caught a quick glance at herself in an antique cheval glass Hazel had given her as a housewarming gift. Her hair was a tangled thatch, and her complexion looked pale and opaque in the early light.

Her heartbeat quickened when she reached for the door that led into the garage. After all, she didn't know what to expect. He could be delirious with fever or even...dead by now, she told herself with grim frankness. She might have something worse than a fugitive on her hands—she might have a fugitive's *body.*

The garage was dark and silent when she opened the door. She slapped at the light switch and the unshaded bulb spilled its waxy, pale light.

Quinn Loudon lay silent and still. Ominously so, she thought as she slowly crossed the garage.

"Mr. Loudon?" she called out tentatively. It was chilly out here, but he looked well bundled in covers. "Quinn?"

Nothing. The only noise was a burst of bird chatter from the yard outside. She felt cold dread slowing her even more.

Yesterday she had placed a rush-bottom chair beside the futon. She settled onto it, studying the peaceful set of his face.

"Can you hear me?"

"Yes, of course," he answered in a wide-awake

voice that made her start so hard the chair creaked under her.

His eyes fluttered open to watch her as he grinned. His voice was weak but clear. "You know, you look beautiful in the morning. I like what you've done to your hair."

"Mr. Loudon, my hair isn't—"

He held up his hand. "This 'Miss Adams' and 'Mr. Loudon' business seems ridiculous now that you've had my pants down. I'm calling you Connie, Connie."

She had to wait a moment for her heart to stop racing. "Call me what you want. But I hardly 'had your pants down' through any choice of my own. Your wound needed tending."

"You even said you could've cut my pants off." He gave her a lazy handsome grin. "That's what they do in the movies."

"I *wish* this were a movie, Mr. Lou—Quinn," she corrected herself a bit reluctantly. She was returning toward the kitchen door as she spoke. "A movie would at least be over in two hours. I'll fix you something to eat."

She quickly filled the coffeemaker and turned it on to brew. Toast and cereal would take care of breakfast, but the cupboard was definitely getting bare. She pulled a strip sirloin out of the freezer to thaw out for later.

Later…here she was planning meals for a fugitive while a multistate manhunt unfolded all around her. Even as she mulled her self-inflicted problem, hollow, reverberating thuds reached her ears.

She hurried to the front door and stepped outside into the cool morning air. The discovery of her Jeep, the day before, had occasioned much stirring and to-do. Now, gazing toward the mountains, she saw the olive-drab helicopter that had started systematically searching the area around the Hupenbecker cabin late yesterday. Time and again the hovering chopper settled on its skids and men poured out to search another grid before moving on.

She wondered, while she took a quick shower, then dressed in matte jersey pants and a knob-button shirt, why no one had been to her house yet to harass her or search the place. Her best guess was that they must believe Loudon had taken to the woods and caves up on the lower slopes.

Once they exhausted that possibility, however, logic told her they'd be paying her a visit.

She managed to eat some toast and marmalade and drink a small glass of juice. Then she fixed a tray and went back out into the garage.

"Can you eat something?" she asked him.

"I better try," he answered, struggling to sit up.

"Here," she told him, folding his pillow behind him to prop him up a little better. "You're pretty weak. It'll be easier if I just feed you. At least I won't have to clean up the mess if you spill."

Settling the pillow, her hand brushed a hard ridge of lateral muscle. His shoulders, too, were taut and muscle-corded—she could see from the way his shirt stretched against them.

"You must play tennis or racquetball?" she guessed.

He shook his head. "I'm a fencing nut. Been into sword duelling ever since I took it up in college. I compete every year at the international tournament in Iwakuni, Japan."

She literally had nothing to say to that. The men she'd met, including at college, were hunters or fishermen or rock climbers. Even one extreme skier. But Mystery Valley didn't attract many sword fighters.

"It sure keeps you in good shape," she observed as she took the bowl of cereal from the tray.

"You have to be. The tournaments combine classic and martial-arts styles. They're gruelling, but exhilarating. Hell, only one thing in this world beats winning a match."

"And what's that? Are you an iron man triathlete as well?" She lifted one eyebrow in skepticism.

"Sex."

"Excuse me?"

"Sex beats it. Of course." He looked at her as if she were a little thick in the head.

A moment passed. A long uncomfortable moment. Connie found her hand trembling.

"Well, here goes..." He opened his mouth.

She lifted the spoon from the bowl. He managed to swallow a few bites of cereal, then he shoved away the spoon so he could speak.

"Listen, I was thinking about it last night. I've *got* to get to Billings, Connie. Will you take me?"

"It's impossible," she told him flatly. "Hear that chopper? It's searching for you. And according to the news, now they're searching every vehicle entering or leaving the valley. We'd never get past the first roadblock."

"I've got to get to Billings," he insisted. "Otherwise I am crisped. There's something I need to get."

"Could—could I get it for you?" she asked reluctantly.

He shook his head. "I wish. But...well, let's just

say it's in a spot where only I or my lawyer, Lance
Pollard, could get it. And I don't doubt for one second
they've got tails on Lance, just waiting for him to go
after anything. He'd be dead five minutes after he laid
hands on it. Just like Cody Anders.''

She watched him in the dim light, fascinated by the
Greco-Roman perfection of his masculine profile, its
aquiline nose, strong jaw, and taut, handsome lips.

He radiated the same impression Doug had: that of
a very attractive man who was quite down-to-earth
about his good looks. Quinn gave the impression as
Doug had, that he was a man of substance, not just
style. But then, she'd been all wrong about Doug,
with disastrous results. Maybe this man, too, racked
up conquests like notches in a gun.

There was no doubt he certainly could if he chose
to.

Again he pushed the spoon away from his mouth.
''Thanks, but I can't eat any more.''

Tiny beads of sweat glistened on his forehead. She
wiped it with a damp sponge. He had seemed fine
when he woke up, but now felt feverish to her touch.

''You're running hot and cold,'' she remarked,
shaking a couple more Tylenols out into her hand.

''Mostly hot,'' he assured her, ''when you get this
close.''

His tone was light. But as he spoke, he raised one
hand and touched three fingertips to the inside of her
arm. That brief, tickling touch was enough, however,
to make a soft warmth spread inside her, accompanied
by a sudden racing of her heart.

''Then maybe I'd better move back,'' she replied,
faking the nonchalance in her tone. Secretly, however,
she felt that her own body was betraying her. Close

proximity to this man was becoming dangerous, threatening her sense of control.

He opened his mouth to say something. But just then a two-tone chime sounded from within the house as someone pressed the bellpush out front.

It was she who froze like a deer in the headlights, not the hunted fugitive.

"No sweat," he told her calmly. "It's your house, so relax. Whoever it is, you can deal with it."

Something in his confident manner rubbed off on her.

"Sin bravely," he added behind her as she headed toward the kitchen door. "Don't miss a beat if whoever it is mentions a search. Just agree on the spot— in fact, act eager to have the place searched. Innocent people usually want to cooperate."

"Are you crazy?"

"Like a fox," he assured her. "Try it."

Constance felt her confidence grow a few more notches when she noticed, through the wide front window in the living room, the Colfax County seal on the door of the Blazer in her driveway.

Constable Ray Lofton waited on the red-brick stoop. He gave her a snaggletoothed grin. Like many year-round residents of Mystery, he had a sanguine complexion from much time spent out of doors.

"Morning, Connie, sorry to bother you so early. I wanted to catch you before you left for work."

Ray seemed somewhat embarrassed as he paused, then added, "I'm under orders, from the U.S. Marshals, to search every house in town. With permission, of course," he added quickly. "I mean, you can refuse and require a warrant."

Don't miss a beat, she reminded herself rapidly.

She held the door open wide. "Sure, come on in, Ray. I'm sorry the place is a little messy. How's Bonnie?"

Ray's wife was editor of the town newspaper, the *Mystery Gazette*. Ray and Bonnie had been classmates with Constance's mom.

"Busy as a one-legged man at a butt-kicking contest," he replied as he stepped past her into the house. "You know her staff writer, Jacquelyn Clayburn, is off on maternity leave. Bonnie has to write all the copy now."

Ray, looking apologetic, accompanied her down the hallway. He glanced only briefly into her bedroom and the spare room she used as an office. He didn't bother with closets or looking under beds.

Quinn was right, she thought. My total cooperation makes Ray feel embarrassed.

"So you think this guy Loudon is actually hiding in town?" Constance asked as Ray headed into the kitchen.

At her question Ray seemed to grow self-conscious with importance.

Despite her nervousness, she had to fight back a grin when he aped the lingo of the federal agents.

"Our intel on Loudon," he assured her officiously, "says he's smart and dangerous. But I'm wondering how smart can he be? I mean, you talk about stupid. The guy steals your Jeep, then drives it back where he started? Brilliant…this guy doesn't even know where he wants to run to. I'll lay two to one odds we nail him in the next twenty-four hours."

So Ray, too, knew that Quinn took her Jeep. Meaning it wasn't held back from the cops, only from the media.

"You're that close to an arrest?" she asked.

He glanced at the door to the garage. "Affirm on that," he replied.

"Excuse me?"

Ray flushed a little as his new jargon tripped her up. "Ahh, yeah, we are. Okay if I peek in the garage, Connie?"

"Of course," she told him in a don't-be-silly tone, in fact almost choking on the words.

So the bluff didn't work after all, she thought in a welter of panic as Ray hit the light switch and poked his head out into the garage.

"Well I'll be darn," he said. "Look at that!"

Her calves went weak as water, and she looked past Ray's stocky bulk. Her old futon was rolled up again, and there was no sign of Quinn Loudon.

"All them for sale signs," Ray chuckled. "Must be a dozen of 'em. You're ambitious, girl."

"'Hitch your wagon to a star,'" she returned lightly, quoting the cover of her high-school yearbook.

"Don't sell the town from under us, that's all I ask."

"Yeah, you and Hazel McCallum," she quipped, nearly blinded with fear.

But relief flooded her when Ray shut the garage door and headed back toward the front of the house.

"Well, hey, thanks, Connie, 'preciate the cooperation. The feds thought, you know, folks would take better to locals bothering them."

"You kidding? It's no bother at all, it makes all of us feel better."

"Give us a call, if you see anything suspicious."

The moment she saw the Blazer rolling down the driveway, Constance returned to the garage.

"Where are you?" she called.

"Behind all these damn signs he was gawking at," Quinn's muffled voice replied, somewhat snappish. "I swear he looked right at me. Wanna help me out of here?"

"I couldn't see you either," she assured him.

Somehow he had managed to squeeze into a cramped space behind the row of slanted signs. Now he was pale and exhausted. The effort had almost been too much for him.

She helped him out from the pile. He was incredibly agile, she thought—one touch would have sent all those signs sliding down.

"You have a real knack for eluding the law," she remarked as she unrolled the futon and helped him back onto it.

She had meant nothing insulting by her comment. But a shadow moved into his face, and the intense, smoke-tinted eyes darkened with something a little wild and reckless—and something worse, perhaps.

Or maybe it was just his weak condition. He was clearly tired and in pain. For a moment he ignored her while he laid himself out on the futon and succumbed to exhaustion.

"I have to make a phone call," she told him. She headed across the garage toward the kitchen door.

"You don't need my permission," he replied in a churlish tone. "It's your house."

"Yes, that's twice you've reminded me now. I know it's my house—I have the payment book to remind me."

"Take me to Billings," he demanded apropos of nothing.

"We'd never make it," she insisted.

He lapsed into a restive silence, and she went inside.

Grabbing the telephone on the bookcase in the living room, she tapped in the number of the real-estate office.

"Mystery Valley Real Estate, Ginny Lavoy speaking."

"Ginny, hey, it's me."

"What's up, Connie?"

Ginny's voice sounded a little strained. That's what happens, Constance lamented, when old regular-as-the-equinox Connie varies in her orbit.

"I think I'll take the day off." She wished she could easily lie, just make up some good excuse: doctor's appointment, PMS, anything. But she had never lied to Ginny in a friendship that went back to childhood, and she wasn't eager to start now.

"Everything okay?" Ginny coaxed.

"You know, I...Ginny, I'm kind of having some strange problems right now. I just need a little personal time I think. It's kind of hard to get into it, but I'll tell you when I get back to the office."

It had never been Ginny's way to pry. In fact, she was one of the most discreet persons Constance had ever known. So it alarmed her when her business partner persisted, "Connie, is...I mean, does this have anything to do with the phone call I got yesterday from the district attorney in Kalispell?"

Alarm prickled her nape. "Ulrick called you? Why?"

"You tell me. He wasn't asking for a date, that's for sure."

"Did he threaten you?" Constance demanded.

"No, not in so many words. He was actually polite

most of the time. When he first identified himself, I thought maybe we had run into some trouble with the credit-background check on the Margolas deal. Remember how I joked how Vincent Margolas looks like a crime syndicate don? Anyway, after just a few questions it was clear Ulrick was asking about the fugitive attorney. Quinn Loudon.''

"What kind of questions?"

"You name it, everything from did you know Loudon before Friday, to, are you an honest person. It was awful. I finally freaked out and just told him I didn't feel comfortable with all the questions."

"How'd he take that?"

"I couldn't tell. He did make his only threatening remark right before he hung up. Something about how a real-estate license isn't carved in stone. Naturally, right after he hung up I thought of a great comeback—neither is the license to practice law. I never think of a good zinger until it's too late. The guy's a bully."

"Trust your first impression," Constance assured her. "Anyhow, I don't have much lined up for today. Can you call the Helzers and reschedule our two o'clock showing?"

"The Helzers, the Helzers...oh, yeah, that's the three-bedroom chateau on Bluebush Road, right? Hey, I can show it if you'd like. I'm free until four anyway."

"Would you, Ginny? I owe you one. And I promise to explain all this as soon as I can."

"You'd better. I'm bursting with curiosity. Just promise you'll be careful? I didn't like that Ulrick guy one bit."

"Promise. Careful as I can be."

Constance hung up the phone, her face blank with

worry. It's hard to be careful, she realized, when someone else is in control and dictating the moves in a game she didn't understand.

It left her no option but reaction.

But nobody made you bring Quinn here, the voice of conscience reminded her. And you can tell him you believe him all you want to. You believed in Doug, too, and look what that got you. Maybe it's time you start to learn from experience.

The expression in her eyes darkened. Her mouth turned in a frown.

Quinn was sleeping well by midmorning, and Constance was starting to feel cabin fever. Realizing she couldn't stay holed up forever, she decided to take care of her postponed shopping.

If the tail was on her again, she couldn't spot it on the moderately busy streets of Mystery. She shopped for groceries, then stopped at Blackford's Bakery for a loaf of fresh seven-grain bread and a half-dozen blueberry muffins.

When she returned home, just past noon, the garage was empty. But she could hear shower noise from the hallway bathroom.

She set her grocery bags on the kitchen table, quickly refrigerating the perishables. Then she went to the bathroom door and tapped on it.

"Quinn?"

The water noise stopped. "Yeah?" He sounded stronger, more alert again.

"What's your trouser size? Is it 34 waist?"

"How'd you guess?"

"Just a hunch," she called in to him. "Hang on a second."

She wasn't sure why she hadn't thrown out—or at least given away—the clothes Doug had left behind. Maybe it was because she had too many closets for one person in her house. She left them hanging where they were, unable to deal with the intimate reminders of him. His clothes in particular were hard for her to face. After all, it was his pleasing exterior that fooled everyone, herself included.

At any rate, it was silly to let Quinn put his dirty clothes back on, complete with bullet holes and bloodstains, when she had perfectly good stuff in his size. She even wondered at the symbolism of letting Quinn dress himself in Doug's facade. Was she hoping she'd be able to dismiss Quinn more easily if he looked like the snake Doug had been? Or was she secretly hoping he'd be able to rise above the fine clothes and prove to be the man Doug wasn't, and could never be?

She selected a dark gray cashmere pullover and triple-pleat gabardine trousers, and even found a pair of Doug's socks rolled up in one of her dresser drawers.

She nudged the bathroom door open. Steam wafted into her face, carrying a vague odor of fresh-scrubbed male.

"Here's some stuff to wear," she called in, eyes carefully averted.

"Bring them on in," he invited.

"I'll set them on the stand by the door," she added, ignoring him. "Just put your laundry in the hamper. I'll wash it."

"Thanks."

Constance made turkey sandwiches and a quick tossed salad while he finished showering and dressing. Her eyes widened in astonishment at the transformed man who limped into the kitchen.

"I tried to keep your nice bandage dry," he greeted her, taking a seat across from her at the kitchen table. "But it got soaked, so I took it off. The wound looks better. I covered it with a gauze pad."

She hardly heard him, his appearance so startled her.

For a moment she regretted giving him the clothing. Even though Quinn looked nothing like Doug, except in build, seeing his clothing all fleshed out again made Doug literally materialize in her kitchen. The impression was vivid and unwelcome.

She slid a plate of sandwiches toward him, averting her eyes.

But he seemed to read the general drift of her thoughts.

"Nice duds. They fit pretty well, too. My compliments to the gentleman's taste. Or the lady who bought them for him."

"The shirt's a little too tight in the shoulders," she observed evasively.

"Maybe you have some other sizes in the stockroom?" he taunted in an exaggeratedly innocent voice while he speared a cherry tomato with his fork.

She felt heat wash into her face. "I'll check my inventory later," she promised coldly.

It was difficult, sitting close to him, to feel anger for very long. Her dominant reaction to his nearness was a consuming sensory awareness of his maleness. Their fingers brushed when she handed him the cruet of vinegar-and-oil, and again her heart raced as unwelcomed illicit sparks arced between them.

"Now that the house has been searched," she told

him, breaking the awkward silence between them, "it'd make more sense if you moved into the spare room. There's no heat out in the garage, and the weather report says it's going to get colder."

"Speaking of getting cold, I caught the news while you were gone. They've pushed the search story way down in priority. Maybe we could make it to Billings now?"

She shook her head. "Helicopters were up in the mountains earlier. Just because the news gets bored with you doesn't mean the law has."

Something in her voice seemed to interest him, and the close scrutiny he gave her disconcerted her.

She stood up and carried their dishes to the sink, setting them on the drainboard. This allowed her to keep her back toward him. And keep the wall up between them.

His voice grew serious. "No, it's not just my 'sexy eyes.' You're taking this risk for other reasons. You remind me of my favorite foster—"

Quinn caught himself. His expression closed.

"Of another woman I knew when I was just a kid. She was just like you. You guess something even before I mention it. How do you do that?"

"I'm not a psychic, if that's your point," she assured him, sidestepping the trail he was following.

"No. But you've figured out the same thing I have. Whoever's following you isn't interested in arresting me."

She said nothing. Her silence was passive confirmation of what he said.

She didn't hear him crossing the kitchen behind her. Suddenly she felt his breath, hot and moist, on the back of her neck. He still radiated shower warmth.

Even the banal fragrance of shampoo and soap couldn't hide the dark male scent of him.

His strong arms encircled her waist.

Her body responded to his touch with a slow, spreading warmth.

"It's not lust that drives you to help me," he said low in her ear. "It's idealism."

Her mind told her to fend off the sexual pass. But again her body rebelled, following its own agenda. Every single contact with him sparked with eroticism. Her heart hammered in her chest.

"Oh, I wouldn't discount lust altogether," she said lightly, though in her soul she knew there was more.

"A guy has to wonder about a woman like you."

His lips brushed her ear as he said this, and he pulled her tighter against him. She was suddenly very aware of his gender—excitedly, dangerously aware.

"A guy has to wonder what?"

"If that deep feeling goes into the bedroom with you, too," he breathed, each word tickling her ear provocatively.

This was the last stand for her feminine resistance. The distrust and hurt left by her experience with Doug flashed strong, throbbing like a knife cut.

Deftly, she ducked sideways, freeing herself from his embrace.

"In the bedroom?" she repeated, her tone bantering. "Of course it does."

"I'll bet with that clear conscience of yours, you sleep like a baby."

She stared at him for a long moment. He met her gaze and held it. Quietly, she answered, "I used to."

He sobered at her words. Grimly, he ran his hand

over his face in a gesture of exhaustion and ambivalence.

Hoping to change the mood, she observed, "You've certainly gotten better. You ought to be able to walk to Billings in another day or two."

"Blame my wonderful nurse. She's as talented as she is beautiful." This time he caught her stare.

She found it too much. She had to look away.

"You're Irish, all right, Quinn Loudon, and you've kissed the Blarney Stone," she retorted in a soft voice.

He stepped closer, and again her body defeated her will by refusing to move.

"You're the one who didn't discount lust," he murmured, his face lowering toward hers.

Her lips parted for his, but the kiss never happened.

Instead she heard gravel crunch under tires in the driveway. She went to the front window. Her heart turned over when she saw the gray sedan.

Chapter 9

"Quinn, my God! That's the car that's been following me."

Staying close to the shadowed walls, Quinn quickly moved enough to glance out through the front window as the driver emerged.

Constance watched his jaw muscle bunch tight when he recognized the man.

"It's Ulrick," he whispered to her. "He's by himself. Play this one just like you did with the constable. You're too disgusted with the whole thing to care, just go ahead and search—that's what you want to convey, got it?"

"But then, I mean, what if he finds you?"

"That's his and my problem, not yours."

That dangerous, reckless glint was back in his eyes, in the defiant set of his features.

Alarm prickled her nape.

"Quinn, don't do something cra—"

"Quiet, girl! When trouble comes, one boss is enough. For now, just do what I say, and you can call me a sexist pig later."

As the doorbell chimed insistently, Quinn hurried down the hallway that led past a bathroom to her bedroom and the spare room.

Her last view of him was his broad shoulders encased in the cashmere polo shirt. She had no opportunity to even see which room he chose to hide in. The chimes sounded again.

With one deep breath, she swung open the door.

"Good morning, Miss Adams. I trust you remember me?"

As if she could easily forget his self-satisfied voice that grated on her nerves despite her apprehension.

With arrogant presumption, Ulrick had already removed his topcoat and folded it over one arm. Again he wore a brown suit, sagging over sloped shoulders, with a light-blue shirt and a navy tie.

"Of course I remember you, Mr. Ulrick. And how could I forget your car? It's been in my rearview mirror since Saturday."

"Anytime you feel harassed," he reminded her, "you need only call the police. That would occur to most women. Unless, of course, they had their own good reasons for being shy about calling the police."

"In a mental hospital, Mr. Ulrick, the sane people have keys on their belts so you can tell them from the inmates. However, it gets more complicated among…legal types. Badges and oaths of office don't always mean much. It's hard to tell the good cops from the bad cops."

An awkward pause ticked by after her comment.

Cold air blew in past him, and she heard the furnace click on.

"May I come in?" he finally asked her.

She flipped the door open wide with careless indifference.

He stepped inside and stopped in the living room, saying nothing.

She made no move farther into the house and did not invite him to sit down. Nor would she after that exchange of venomous bites on the front porch.

She recalled Quinn's advice and seized the initiative. "You have my permission to search the place, Mr. Ulrick. Ray Lofton already searched it earlier, but go right ahead and, what's the jargon, 'toss' the place. You obviously don't trust me, or you wouldn't be following me."

If he had come to search, however, he was in no hurry to begin.

"It's not so much you I don't trust, Miss Adams. It's Quinn Loudon. The man has an incredible ability to...manipulate others to his purpose. Especially women," he added significantly.

"Oh, I see. Loudon is an unscrupulous Don Giovanni, and you are only following me to protect my virtue."

She hadn't intended to deliberately antagonize him. But her strong dislike for the man got the better of her.

For a moment his sharp little fox-terrier face flushed pink with anger. Hazel had a phrase for men like him: all wood and no sap.

"Scorn is easy, Miss Adams, when you don't know all the facts. Loudon has a history of creating sympathy in women and then exploiting them for his purposes. Especially women who fit a particular psychological profile. A psychiatrist, who was on the staff at Child Protective Services in Albany, New York, spotted it when he was only fourteen.''

Child Protective Services...

She recalled Dolph Merriday speaking on the radio, his comment that both Quinn's parents were career criminals.

''Spotted what?'' she asked, curiosity overcoming her skepticism.

''His abnormal need to control women, a result of long periods of early-childhood abandonment by his parents, especially his mother. Both of his parents were drug addicts, you know. Loudon has since developed remarkable talent for recognizing a certain type of woman—and for literally enthralling them.''

''Enthralling?'' she repeated. ''That's rather Victorian, isn't it? Does he bite their necks, too?''

He ignored her barb and thrust one of his own. ''He's especially adept at gaining the trust of women who, practical and intelligent on the social surface, have a fatal weakness for placing trust in all the wrong people, romantically speaking.''

You smirking bastard, she thought, doing a slow burn. You prying, meddling scoundrel. It was obvious he had pumped someone locally and learned about Doug. She was still fuming over his invasion of her private life when his next question hit her like a bucket of cold water.

''Where is Loudon right now, Miss Adams?''

Technically speaking, at that moment she really didn't know exactly where he was.

So she looked him boldly in the eye. ''I don't know,'' she answered.

"If you did know, would you tell me?"

"No."

He laughed. "I already know that about you, Miss Adams. In fact, that's my point. With his good looks and manners, Loudon can play a certain type of woman just like a piano. But need I remind you to look beyond the charm? Quinn Loudon fired on U.S. Marshals. He's a killer."

Despite her aversion to Ulrick, some of his points did trouble her. She had met a few charming manipulators in her professional life, too, not just her love life, and Ulrick was right—solid credentials and polished manners were sometimes mere shields for crooks and con artists.

"You act as if I'm defending him, Mr. Ulrick. I'm not. I just don't understand your tactics. Such as following me around and even harassing my co-worker, Ginny Lavoy."

"I did not 'harass' her."

"Well, I think you did, and you're harassing me, too. Isn't it quite abnormal for a prosecutor to take such an…active role in a case? After all, I'm a witness and a victim here. Not the criminal."

"Who told you how a prosecutor should act?" he challenged.

She laughed at his pomposity. "Nobody had to tell me. I'm not six years old. Mr. Ulrick, in the real-estate business one has to deal with lawyers all the time. And spend a surprising amount of time in court watching them work. The lawyers I've known rely on detectives, police or private, for this door-to-door stuff."

The entire time she spoke, Ulrick was staring past

her at the drainboard. She followed his insectile gaze. Her stomach lurched.

He saw two coffee cups, two saucers, two sandwich plates, two salad bowls.

His accusing eyes cut back to her face. "There's an old saying, 'the cobbler should stick to his last.' Frankly, Miss Adams, you are not qualified to make legal judgments."

Again, feeling her deep loathing for the man, she realized how much she wanted Quinn to be in the right, despite the terrible danger that would place her in. It didn't mean she condoned all of his actions— right or wrong, there was still something reckless and dangerous about an attorney who could turn "gang buster" in a heartbeat and shoot up a courtroom to "get out of town."

"I'm not too uneducated to notice you aren't recording this conversation today like you did on Saturday. That's because your friend Mumford isn't here, isn't it? Because this visit wasn't meant to be part of the official record, was it?"

"I can assure you of one thing, Miss Adams. This is *not* 'door-to-door' stuff—you have police canvassing in mind when you say that. I'm not canvassing— yours is the only door I've come to."

"You'll excuse me, I'm sure, if I don't pretend to be flattered, Mr. Ulrick."

For the first time, his inspection lingered on her body, too.

"Perhaps," he suggested, his tone thick with innuendo, "you find Quinn Loudon desirable? But let me tell you, he's a liar and a user. You'd do well to reassess your trust...and put it in someone who won't abuse it...or you."

She stepped around him and returned to the door, opening it wide. "Get out," she told him in a tone of controlled anger.

He laughed, forcing it a little. But something in her manner did evidently intimidate him because he headed for the door.

"I don't think you're harboring Loudon here— right now," he qualified, giving the dishes another glance. "I talked to Ray Lofton, and I'm satisfied he searched well."

Good for you, Ray, she thought.

"But I do think you're actively aiding and abetting him somehow," he added.

He opened the door, and cold air licked at her like an icy tongue—the temperature was finally lowering to Montana norms.

He turned and said, "I'll warn you one last time, Miss Adams. In the eyes of the law, those who hold a candle for the devil are doing the devil's work."

"If that were true," she flung after him, "the law would have to arrest itself."

Despite her belief that Quinn was telling her the truth, Constance couldn't completely discount everything Ulrick had said about the fugitive's supposed talent at "manipulating women." After all, she knew little about Quinn or his past.

Doubts lingered, like an unsettling odor in the house, even after the prosecutor had left.

She took care to avoid any potential for the physical intimacy they had begun to share before Ulrick's arrival. More than ever she began to feel the urgency of her plight. She was hiding a man, in her home, who could not possibly escape from Mystery any time soon. And he was here by her choice, her own reckless actions, not his.

Such thoughts, however, invariably recalled the sizzle each time his skin touched hers. And she knew *that* was the real danger she feared: the way the fire in his dark eyes struck answering flames within her.

So she kept the kitchen table between them while she reported her conversation with Ulrick. She didn't gloss over his remarks about "enthralling" and "manipulating" women.

Quinn's face seemed more resigned than angry, as if he expected nothing less from Ulrick.

"Technically," he told her, "Ulrick has the legal right to investigate, since he's a sworn officer of the court holding jurisdiction. But you caught him dead to rights about the recorder—this was no official visit. I just hope you'll remember the danger of pushing these guys too far. Ulrick has access to some thugs to do his dirt work. His kind always do."

Again, Quinn gave her nothing about his past, and nothing about the way Ulrick kept bringing it up. Indecision plagued her. She couldn't help thinking about her reckless choice to bring Quinn here. Never mind how odious she found Ulrick—he just *might* be onto something regarding Quinn's...hold over women, his ability to somehow make his purpose their own. Clearly he wanted to get away, and just as clearly he needed someone—her?—to help him do it.

She decided she had to say something.

"Quinn? Before Ulrick came, you mentioned a woman you knew from childhood."

"Still know, actually."

"Do you mean an adopted mother?"

His face seemed to close in against her. "No, a foster mother," he replied matter-of-factly.

"Ulrick and Merriday, they both dwell so much on your childhood and your parents—your real parents, I mean. Why?"

He looked at her with eyes as defiant as his tone. "Kind of obvious, isn't it? Because being the son of criminals and addicts is a quick and easy way to establish my criminal pedigree, to make me stand out as dangerous by birth. You know the line, 'Happy families are all alike.'"

"But 'every unhappy family is unhappy in its own way,'" she finished for him.

He nodded. "Automatically marks me out as a weirdo, antisocial. That's important because they don't want any attention on the real focus of this mess—bribes and kickbacks in the road-construction business. Not to mention Anders' strange disappearance. They also don't mention the fact that I was only charged with attempted bribery. They don't even want those words whispered—they're so benign. So instead, they make me into a monster. They harp away at my bad character and my notorious background."

She hoped he would volunteer more. Instead, he withdrew inside of himself, partly, she suspected, from lingering exhaustion. Even though his fever was under control now, he was still weak and tired.

"C'mon back in the spare room and get some rest," she told him, rising from the table.

He nodded, following her down the hallway. She had converted the front section of the spare bedroom into her home office: A station for her computer and printer, a shelf of reference works, business software, and county plat-books showing the official boundaries of all properties in Colfax County. Along the back wall was a twin bed with an old chenille spread.

"The bed's nothing fancy," she apologized, "but you'll be more comfortable in here—a floor vent near the bed controls the heat."

Despite his evident exhaustion, Quinn's gaze was immediately drawn to an enchanting oil painting over the bed. It depicted golden moonbeams reflecting like liquid jewels from ocean waves.

"That's fine work," he complimented. "Yours?"

"Don't I wish. I don't paint, but I love the art form. I bought that in Paris at a modern-art auction The Louvre sponsors every summer. After paying for it, I practically had to hock my jewels to pay my hotel bill, but I had to have it. The artist told me it was inspired by the First Movement of Beethoven's Moonlight Sonata."

"Sounds like you're quite the devotee."

"I am, and I dreamed of being a great painter when I was little. But I must confess I also make money investing in art."

"Collecting it, you mean?" He nodded toward the oil painting.

"Mm-hm. But that one's not on the market and never will be. It's just personal gratification."

His eyes seized hers, and she felt her breath snag in her throat.

"Nothing wrong with personal gratification," he assured her.

She pretended she hadn't heard him, waiting a moment until she could trust her voice. "Art is always a smart investment because the real stuff can only gain in value over time."

Beneath the surface of her commonplace remark,

she felt a simmering tension—as if her mouth sent one message but the rest of her body another. The way he stared at her didn't help her composure any.

"I—I do it more for fun than to get rich," she added to end the awkward silence, barely managing to tear herself from the powerful hold of his eyes. "It gives me an excuse to splurge on trips to the famous galleries."

She paused, noticing his assessment of her. "You look surprised? Did you expect everyone in Mystery to collect porcelain knick-knacks?"

He shrugged, bemused eyes measuring the careful distance she was keeping between them. "It's a side of you that doesn't show immediately—I mean, rural real-estate hustler and all."

A shadow crossed his face, and she busied herself in clearing some boxes of office supplies off the bed.

Quinn studied the painting, but only with his eyes. In his heart he battled the same secret fear he'd felt every time he tried to get close to a woman he admired: they were silk purses, and he was a sow's ear trying to fake it.

His inner turmoil had actually begun earlier with her offhand comment about his "knack for eluding the law." And obviously Ulrick's visit had planted seeds of doubt within her.

She'd be an idiot *not* to have doubts about me, he realized. Her obviously solid, small-town roots, her secure and interesting, full life…this very painting, even, all served to throw a spotlight on his own criminal behavior these past few days. He was far worse than simply one of the hoi polloi…not just common, but a common *criminal*. At least in her eyes, and maybe even in his own.

"There, all ready," she said, turning away from the bed to look at him. Again their eyes met, held, and suddenly she seemed very aware of the bed's proximity to them. She sent him a nervous little smile.

"A dimple on the chin means a devil within," he told her, tone light, but eyes caressing her like hands against her bare flesh.

"So I've heard. You have one, too."

"Well, there you go—we have a common ancestor in Satan. We should get married and protect the bloodline. Raise little hellions all over the place."

They both laughed, momentarily relieving the tension. But joke or not, the reference to "bloodline" briefly brought the shadow back into his face.

"Sleep well," she told him, heading for the door. For a moment, as she stepped past him, she was sure he started to raise his arms—as if to stop her.

Her heart raced. If he did, she wondered what she would do about it—stay or resist.

But she never had to make that choice. His arms returned to his side. He let her pass by, and turned away from her with a simple, automatic, "Thank you, Connie, I will."

"Connie, when I called your office and Ginny told me you took a personal day? I had to sit right down, it unsettled me so much."

Her mother's voice seemed to yammer in her ear. Constance had caught the phone during its first ring, hoping it hadn't awakened Quinn. It was late on Monday afternoon, a wedge of brittle winter sunshine slanting through the wide front window. It turned the hardwood floor the color of luminous honey.

"With Quinn Loudon still loose and in this area,"

Dorothy pressed on, "why, I nearly panicked. You *never* take a personal day like this. Vacations, sure, but those are always planned. Never a day off like this. And I just saw you yesterday. You never mentioned—"

"Mom, please, at least pause to breathe! You know how you can get all wound up over nothing. Look, what's the big deal if I take a day off? At my job, I'm the boss, remember?"

"Of course you can take time off. Don't be silly. But it's just—with Quinn Loudon still—"

"I know, *I know,* you've said it several times now." She paused, letting the first wave of irritation pass. "Mom, the whole town is acting like Quinn Loudon is Godzilla or something. Anyway, he's probably up in the mountains. He's not after anyone around here. He's just running from the law. He's not some mad slasher chanting my name."

"All I know is what I'm told. And Ray Lofton told me he's searching house to house."

"Uh-huh, he searched mine already, and you know he did. You also know how Ray loves playing things up a little, too. Mom, Quinn Loudon can't be here in town. He's not invisible. So just calm down."

"You've got good locks there?"

"You know they're better than yours. Dead bolts."

"Well...but why *did* you take a day off?"

Sudden exasperation, and the underlying entanglements of the web she was weaving, make Constance snap back, "That's why they're called personal days."

"You don't have to use that tone," her mother censured her.

"Tone? What about yours? I'm not in high school

anymore. Speaking of which—Beth Ann uses a 'tone' with you all the time, and she gets away with it."

"Not in front of your dad, she doesn't."

"Oh, great, you stand up to her only when Dad's there to back you? *That'll* teach Beth to respect women, all right."

"What in the world got you on this subject?"

Her mother sounded confused by the sudden shift in topic.

Constance berated herself for picking on her. In a more patient voice, she went on, "Never mind. Dad's not the issue, anyway, I'm talking about me and you. I'm twenty-eight years old and in charge of my own life."

"Did I ever say—"

"Mom, look, I'm sorry, I'm just not in the mood right now for a big production over the phone. I'm fine, okay? Really. I'll talk to you later. Love you."

She hung up before she really let loose on her mother. Constance knew she was just naturally worried about her oldest child. But maternal "hovering" was especially irksome when she already had enough stress to handle.

When the phone on the bookcase rang again only a few seconds after she'd hung up, she angrily speared the handset from its cradle, expecting her mother again.

"Mom, please, I just don't—"

"If *I* was your mother," Hazel's throaty voice cut her off, "you'd be standing tall in the wood shed right about now, missy."

"Hazel! I'm sorry, I thought...why in heaven would I be standing tall?"

"Why? You tell me. You can begin by telling me

why federal agents just paid me a visit about the Hupenbecker cabin?''

''They—they did?''

''Honey, didn't I just say they did? A corn-fed young FBI fellow who looks like Elliot Ness constipated, and some mealymouthed D.A. who needs to eat his Wheaties. Now we've got that point established, you tell me *why?*''

''Well…see, you own the cabin.''

''Well, cut off my legs and call me Shorty! I didn't know that. Listen, girl, you stop bamboozling me because you're no good at it like I am. This weak-sister D.A., Ulrick, he bawled like a bay steer. Asked did I know Quinn Loudon, asked did I know you and what was my opinion of your character?''

Constance swallowed the hard lump in her throat. ''What did you tell him?''

''Tell him? Why, that you're a hell-raising whore nicknamed Mattress Mary.''

''Oh, that ought to clear me,'' she winced.

''Shame on you for thinking Hazel McCallum lets *any*body push her around in Mystery Valley. Or any of her neighbors. I told him to stick his questions where the sun doesn't shine. This Ulrick is a toad, and I'll squash him yet. But I can't help you until you tell me everything, Connie. The whole thing, from soup to nuts.''

''Well, to be honest, I've been wanting to tell you.''

''That's the girl. Stop wanting and do it.''

Connie hesitated. Her paranoia flared. Certainly it occurred to her that her phone could be bugged, but she would have to take the chance. She really needed someone to talk to.

"You already know about Friday, when Quinn Loudon called and lied about wanting to buy the cabin. And what happened Saturday when I was followed back to Mystery and you and I found the cabin left wide open."

"Right, pick it up from there."

Methodically, beginning with the way she shook the tail on Sunday, she hit all the important points: finding Quinn at the cabin and taking him home with her; fooling Ray Lofton; then Ulrick's visit. Finally she explained Quinn's desperation to reach Billings and obtain some kind of evidence he claimed might clear him.

Hearing it all from her own mouth made Constance despair of her actions.

"Oh, Hazel," she breathed into the phone, suddenly feeling the saline sting of pent-up tears. "Am I *worse* than a fool? Should I call the police right now?"

"Connie, what is wrong with you and what doctor told you so?"

"What—what do you mean?"

"All these years around my bad influence, and you're still being so milk-kneed? Just tell me this, do you believe him or not? Believe that his life really might be in danger?"

"I—"

"Don't start with 'I.' Start with yes or no."

Constance laughed, sniffling a little at the same time. She raised her legs up onto the sofa and hugged her knees to quell her trembling. "Yes, I believe him."

"I already knew that much. It's in your tone every time you speak about this young fellow."

"It is?"

"Mm…among other things."

"Yeah, well. Not to throw it in your face, Hazel, but you said something similar about Doug."

"Throw it in my face," Hazel scoffed. "A Mc-Callum doesn't flinch from her own screwups. And I'll tell you something else—we don't quit riding all horses because some are biters."

Hazel became practical again. "What is this evidence he has in Billings?"

"He won't tell me. Says it's not safe for me to know so much."

"Well, if the rest of his tale is true, that shines right by me. Especially…let me just ask you. Is he notching his sight on you?"

Again Constance laughed. "You mean, is he interested?"

"Of course he's 'interested.' He's a man under ninety, and my God, look at you. That face and body of yours comprise a traffic hazard. What I mean is, does he act like he has more than just hot pants for you? And you for him?"

That question, in slightly less blunt terms, had been plaguing her ever since Ulrick's visit earlier.

"I don't know. Maybe," she replied.

"How 'bout the fear? Can you handle that?"

"As long as I'm convinced he's telling the truth, yes."

"All right, then," Hazel told her in a brisk, no-nonsense voice. "Roll the bones, baby."

Constance wasn't sure she'd heard her right. "What?"

"Shoot the dice! Take a chance, and get that strapping, good-looking son of a gun to Billings."

"You mean it, don't you?"

"Why, no one's called me senile yet. Of course I mean it. Young lady, this valley is humming with excitement since last Friday. We haven't had any real action around here since Ike Knoblaugh got drunk and rolled his cattle truck."

"But...I mean, you've seen the helicopter and heard about the roadblocks. How would we—"

"Never mind all that for now. I'll run my traps," Hazel assured her—her phrase for gathering information from her secret sources. "We'll cook up something. For now, keep Quinn hidden and don't let that young hothead go off the rails. Also, keep a very close eye on this Ulrick fellow. Something's got him all wound up to a fare-thee-well, and he's scared enough to do almost anything."

Chapter 10

Day gave way to night, and while Quinn slept on, Constance had plenty of time to worry—especially about how she was going to tell Quinn that Hazel, too, was now in on his secret.

She watched the last rosy flush of sunlight bleed from the sky. The temperature outside had begun to plunge rapidly, starting in late afternoon as a front blew down from Alberta. She finally stirred herself from her spot near the huge front window, going into the hallway to set the thermostat a little higher.

The furnace clicked on, and for a moment she stood over the floor vent in the hall, letting the heat caress her and quell her trembling.

Feeling a little warmer now, she brewed herself a mug of chamomile tea and tried to work on her laptop computer in the living room.

But it was futile; she simply couldn't concentrate.

It was impossible to keep her mind from straying to thoughts of the man sleeping in her house.

His touch, earlier, still tingled against her skin, as did the image of his lips parting to accept hers in a kiss that was interrupted by Ulrick.

The entire situation, she reminded herself in dazed disbelief, began last Friday—only three days ago. But they'd been through so much together that the intensity of their experience cut through the usual protocols and rituals—cut right to the essential problem of passion between a man and a woman.

Such thoughts still dominated her mind when she went to bed around eleven.

Strange, illogical dreams plagued her uneasy sleep.

They would always begin, pleasantly enough, with her and Quinn alone at the Hupenbecker cabin, cozy and warm. But each pleasant dream always turned bizarre, starting when Quinn would just suddenly be wearing Doug's clothing. Somehow she'd end up in a homeless shelter, receiving huge credit-card bills for Quinn's romps with his arm candy.

Quinn...Doug...

She woke up around 2:00 a.m., not sure, for a few confused moments, just who was sleeping across the hall from her. Or if anyone at all was there.

The house was silent and chilly, the only sound the winter wind rustling the treetops outside. She could see a patina of moonlit frost on her window.

Gooseflesh pebbled her bare arms when she got up and pulled a terry-cloth robe on over her chemise. She went into the hallway and nudged the thermostat another two degrees higher.

She was about to go back to bed when the slanted-open door of the spare room caught her eye, and she paused, listening.

She could hear his breathing, steady and peaceful. Good. He hadn't slept this long since Thursday and needed the rest.

For no required reason, she pushed the door open a few more inches and peeked into the room.

It was always warmer in this room than in the rest of the house, and Quinn had shucked the covers off in his sleep. His naked body lay partially exposed, like a study in shadow and light. Winter moonlight gleamed on him, his precisely sculpted muscles relaxed yet still powerfully defined in his calves, thighs, back, and outstretched arms.

In those first moments she literally forgot to breathe. The lines and forms of his body, in the frosted lighting, made as perfect an artwork as any she'd ever seen.

She lingered there, unwilling to close the door on this vision of masculine perfection.

Somehow, after perhaps thirty seconds, she must have sensed that he knew she was there.

"Connie?" he mumbled.

She should have at least felt embarrassment about being caught at voyeurism. But she felt the odd conviction that this moment was inevitable and beyond her will or his.

"Yes?" she answered in a soft voice little more than a whisper.

He made no effort to conceal his nakedness. He rose up on one elbow to watch her in the ghostly moonlight.

"Well—are you coming in or not?"

She said nothing. The spare room was small, a

postage stamp, really. But the miles to cross it to his bed was too far a distance.

She met his eyes, her heart pounding like a tympanum.

"So is it lust or something deeper?" he growled.

"According to you I saved your life."

The suffused moonlight emphasized his prominent cheekbones and the strong angularity of his face. "Why did you save my life?"

"Fate?" she whispered. "Eventuality? Something deeper."

He stood. With two long strides, he crossed the vast expanse between them.

She could hardly look at him, at his nudity, his hunger.

He took her hand and pulled her toward him. The door closed behind her. Her robe untied as if by itself, and he pulled it off, letting it fall in a puddle around her feet. Only the sheer silk chemise covered her.

"No, please wait," she murmured, unsure of herself and the fiery need that had sparked within her.

"Then stay right there in the moonlight." He eased his nude form back onto the bed. "Just stay like that. Let me look at you. Just for a moment."

She stood still. His stare seemed like a ravenous animal, greedy and obsessed. Despite the heat of his eyes, the room felt cold and inhospitable. She shivered and covered her barely-clad chest with her arms.

Quinn reached for her. His strong, sensitive hands slid slowly up her thighs and under the chemise. They paused to cup the supple swell of her hips.

She trembled, her legs weakening when he slid both hands across her stomach and took a breast in each hand. He stiffened her nipples in slow, circular strokes that sapped even more strength from her legs.

She moaned with shameless abandon as he slid the silk garment off and folded her into the bed beside him and placed her in the nest of the warm spot he'd just vacated. Their bare legs intertwined, and he pulled her closer, his aroused sex hard and heavy as he pressed against her still-cool skin.

"Quinn," she whispered, tangling her trembling fingers in his hair and turning his face to hers.

He kissed her, silencing her, his tongue exploring. Over and over she whispered his name as he kissed and tasted her body, lighting fires everywhere he touched.

His own need intensified with hers. His mouth on the tip of her breast became more and more needy. His tongue sizzled across each of her full nipples, giving her small spikes of pleasure she could feel even through her back.

Finally she felt one of his hands slide between her thighs, then move higher. Several fingers gently probed, opening her soft folds like petals to sunlight, sending currents of pleasure pulsing through her.

"I want you," he whispered.

He rolled on top of her and pushed his length inside her, whispering incoherent words of electric pleasure. Groaning her name, he slid both hands underneath her, thrusting her up so he could enter even deeper, filling her.

The furnace, humming quietly to life, nudged the curtain into rippling motion. The moonlight danced on them just as it danced across waves in the painting hanging above them.

Again, then again, she heard herself cry out, felt

her long-hungry body lifting, peaking, each climax stronger than the one before it. With Quinn she'd found a rhythm more joyous than she'd ever experienced before, and the act was more than lust and sex. It was pent-up need, the sheer desperation of their plight; it was a way to get lost, to forget.

Again and again in him she was absorbed in pure, mindless pleasure so intense the world fell away and lay crumpled at her feet.

Her efficient inner clock woke Constance at seven o'clock sharp, as it did almost every weekday.

Even before her eyelids opened, however, she recognized the signs of a near-sleepless night: aching eyes, sluggishness, bodily weariness and exhaustion.

But the arms and legs entwined with hers were pleasantly new and unfamiliar in a safe, dreamlike way. Still floating in the misty haze between sleeping and waking, she snuggled against the human warmth beside her.

Human warmth....

Human warmth?

Her eyes snapped open, and she came fully awake.

Of all the things she might have worried about, she realized before anything else: I've slept with Quinn. The outlaw. The desperado.

Chasing this thought, she carefully extricated herself from Quinn's embrace. Almost in shock, she wondered what had gotten into her last night, and how she was going to handle the new situation she had created. It was already complicated enough before she gave in to her lust.

No, not lust. It was more than lust—on her part, anyway.

Even knowing so little about him, she had felt something inside her soul connecting with his. What she had felt, when he was inside her, was far more meaningful and fulfilling than mere sated desire.

But, she rebuked herself, that doesn't mean *he* feels the same.

At this reminder, harsh reality came crashing in on her. Roger Ulrick's troubling remarks yesterday, and unpleasant thoughts of Doug, were blunt reminders that she was the world's worst judge of men and their character.

Quinn sighed, muttering something in his sleep, but he didn't quite wake up when she eased out of bed, naked and shivering in the gray morning light.

Ice coated the windows. She picked up her chemise and slipped her robe on, then crossed the hallway to her bedroom.

She folded open the louvered doors of the big closet and selected a white pullover sweater, indigo pants, and a pair of shearling-lined suede boots. She grabbed underclothing from a bureau drawer, then placed everything ready on her bed.

A steaming-hot shower, in the smaller bathroom off the master bedroom, was followed by a fast, brutally cold rinse in an attempt to jolt herself awake.

Among the day's many problems still awaiting resolution, she wasn't sure what to do about work—whether to go or not.

Best to get ready just in case, she decided. She could hear Quinn stirring around as she dressed and quickly applied makeup at her triple-mirror vanity. A nervous stirring in her stomach reminded her, yet again, that she still had to tell him about Hazel.

Guilt stabbed at her. Never mind that he was the

fugitive. He had trusted her, after all, and she had broken faith with him. Anyway, that's how he would see it.

Thus ruminating, she nearly dropped her hairbrush when he knocked on her door.

"Are you hiding?" His tone, muffled by the closed door, was meant to be ironic, she guessed.

Nonetheless, it also revealed confusion.

"It's open," she called out. She pivoted on her chair to smile at him—albeit a bit awkwardly—as he entered her room.

He wore the trousers she had given him but no shirt. For a moment, seeing the buff, sculpted torso, she felt a thrill of excitement, a tickling flutter of desire.

He met her gaze. His lips coaxed into a smile.

"You looked like a Greek goddess last night, naked in that moonlight," he said, still standing just inside the door.

The sincerity and longing in his tone made her flush with pleasure at the compliment. But the reckless, remote glint was back in his eyes, reminding her she still had news to break to him.

It wasn't easy to find a natural opening. He, too, had plenty to think about besides the pleasures of the bed.

She watched him cross to the west window, staying off to one side, and peek out past the curtains. He studied the yard carefully, patiently.

"Going to work?" he asked her, still watching outdoors.

"What would you suggest? I mean, until we—"

She caught herself, momentarily nonplused at how

readily she was melding their lives, as if they were a couple.

"Until you have a plan," she corrected herself, "I thought it might be a good idea to go in to the office."

He nodded. "Yeah, you're right. They're watching you, at least sometimes, and you've already missed a day. Best not to disrupt your normal schedule. Connie?"

"Yes?"

He turned from the window to look at her. Even in that grainy light, she thought, he's strikingly handsome.

"Speaking of disruptions," he said, "I really am sorry for tossing a monkey wrench into your life. I didn't think last night would play out the way it did."

"Yes." She didn't know what else to do but agree.

"Are you...sorry about last night?"

"Are you?" she returned his question in a soft voice.

He shook his head, not one sign of hesitation. "Nope, not even if you are."

His voice seemed sincere to her, but some troublesome qualifier glinted through the smoky tint of his eyes. Either he was staring at inner demons, she thought, or he's a superb actor. Despite plenty of experience to suggest the latter, she chose to believe it was demons.

"Quinn?" She turned to the mirror again and began brushing her hair behind her ears.

"Hmm?"

She secured her hair with silver barrettes, hands trembling slightly. "I have something to tell you."

Something in her tone must have alerted him. She saw his face in the mirror, wary now.

"Don't tell me you're late?"

She laughed, but did some quick math in her head just for future reference. They sure as hell didn't go to the drugstore the night before. She might have taken on more trouble than she knew even now.

"Look," she blurted out awkwardly, "you need to get to Billings, right?"

"Like a shark needs the ocean, lady."

"I—well, that is, a very good friend of mine is working on a plan for us—I mean you—"

Even in the mirror she saw the expression in his eyes turn dark and angry like a sudden squall. He took two steps toward her, and for a moment fear lanced through her.

"You told someone about me?"

"You don't understand," she insisted. "It's my friend Hazel McCallum, she—"

"McCallum? The cattle rancher?"

"Yes."

"Why not alert the media while you're at it? Governor Collins considers that old woman to be a Western icon. He actually killed the big federal project to dam Mystery Valley as a reservoir, all on her say-so."

"All right, and I'm telling you she's my best friend. Quinn, she supports you. She even encouraged me to help you when I—when I expressed some doubts. She says she thinks you're innocent."

His eyes sought hers, then held them. "How 'bout those doubts of yours?"

"They don't concern your innocence," she assured him, truthful yet evasive.

He mulled everything, his face troubled. "I can use

some competent help," he finally conceded. "When did you tell her?"

"Yesterday afternoon while you were asleep."

"If she wanted me arrested, it would be done by now."

"Exactly. If you have faith in me, then believe me, you can have faith in Hazel. Her word is her bond."

"Oh, I have faith in you, all right."

She believed him. But that troubled glint was back in his eyes. Despite the need in his soul, he seemed unable to accept what she offered. Something stood between him and happiness, some secret that plagued him like a family curse.

"We'd better have some breakfast," she suggested. "Then I'll call Hazel and tell her I'll be at work if she wants to call me."

He nodded.

She stood up, and only inches separated them.

His hands reached for her. They embraced. For a few moments, while she moved her hands in slow circles on his muscle-corded back, the exquisite memory of making love to him consumed her.

"You *would* have to be all dressed," he complained in her ear as he kissed it until her heart was racing.

"Five more seconds of that," she protested, gently pushing him away, "and I won't be dressed."

"Would that be so awful?"

His eyes and tone challenged her to deny her hunger for more pleasure. That spreading warmth was back in her loins, giving the lie to any verbal denial she might make.

"Awful?" she repeated, flashing him a demure smile. "No, and that's precisely why I'd better not.

So tell me, are you in the mood…for apple pancakes?'' she teased him.

"Wrong appetite,'' he assured her. "Let's try another.''

But she deftly ducked around him. "One thing about you men—you're simple and direct when it comes to your loins.''

A true fencer, he parried immediately, "Would you prefer a dash of treachery and deceit?''

Resentment flared up within her instantly. She moved to the doorway, stopping to turn and glower back at him. He saw the hurt in her angry amber eyes.

"Men already provide plenty of that,'' she informed him with cold precision. "I'll fix us something to eat before I go to work.''

Willing herself to concentrate on business, not on Quinn Loudon, Constance opened the real-estate office promptly at nine o'clock.

Ginny took every Tuesday morning off to volunteer as a teacher's aide at her daughter's elementary school in nearby Whiteford Township. Constance was grateful she was gone—she was in no mood to explain a still-unfolding situation she couldn't even grasp herself, let alone make clear to someone else.

For about forty-five minutes she actually succeeded in proofreading copy for some local listings she had sent to a real-estate magazine that served Colfax County. Her calendar included a ten o'clock appointment to show a place out on Indian School Road—a beautiful five-bedroom log home with a wraparound porch.

She locked up the office at 9:45, grateful she had worn her long wool coat—it was cold outside and getting colder. She watched each breath form airborne ghosts as she walked out to the car.

If Ulrick or anyone else was following her, she couldn't spot them as she left the outskirts of Mystery Township. She bore south on the winding two-lane asphalt road that led to a vocational-skills school for the Flathead Indian tribe.

A car already waited in the cul-de-sac out front when Constance arrived at the house. Stuart Beals and his wife stood on the porch, looking cold and miserable despite their ridiculously heavy winter coats, scarves, and gloves.

Beals, a Southerner, had evidently done well for himself in the restaurant-equipment business. Now he desired a second home out West. She had picked up bad vibes from him over the phone, especially his tendency toward one-upmanship.

Constance escorted them through the place, pointing out such features as the gorgeous custom mill-work throughout, custom built-in bookcases, the large breakfast area with built-in buffet.

Despite her sleep deprivation, momentary memories of last night, in bed with Quinn, abruptly energized her body and mind. But recalling his searing kisses and touch also lent an absurd feel to her professional patter.

"As you can see," she told them, escorting them into the huge den, "this room has lots of windows and bookcases."

"Awfully tall ceiling," Stuart Beals pointed out. He was middle-aged, florid-faced from the cold outside, a prissy, nondescript little man who wielded his success like a bludgeon. Pamela Beals, in stark contrast, was gracious and self-effacing, quick to smile.

"Ceilings this high," Beals added, "cost a small fortune to heat in winter."

Constance tried to stay focused on the here and now. Again, however, she saw torrid images from last night, felt Quinn's hands under her chemise, firing her body like a kiln.

"You...you might be pleasantly surprised about that," Constance managed to assure him. She pointed at twin skylights. "Those are solar-assist panels. Notice how we can't see our breath in this room even though the heat is off? The master bedroom has them, too."

During all this, Pamela Beals had been gazing through the windows at the terraced garden out back, complete with a three-tier marble fountain.

"I just love that gazebo, Stuart," she interjected. "It's two stories. Isn't that cute?"

Constance watched him send his wife a warning glance. It was a look she'd noticed often in the real-estate game. Prospective buyers like Beals felt compelled to engage in certain rituals of bargaining. One was the maxim: *Never show too much enthusiasm; they'll jack up the price.*

"A gazebo," Beals announced primly, "means much less to me than proximity to a good golf course."

It was hard to be focused and professional when her calves were going weak at the memory. In her mind's eye Constance felt Quinn's fingers coaxing her open. *I can feel how much you want me....*

All at once she realized both of them were watching her with expectant faces, waiting for her to say something....oh, right, golf.

"Valley Greens is only fifteen minutes from here,"

Constance somehow managed to point out. "Eighteen holes with a full-service restaurant and clubhouse."

"What about tennis courts?" he demanded.

"There's several at the park downtown."

"Clay or asphalt?" he forged on.

"I'm really not sure," she confessed, not giving a tinker's damn.

Beals sent his wife a smug glance. *See there? Caught her, didn't I?*

"The schools in this township, elementary and secondary, rate among the highest in the nation," she informed them. "I have the exact ranking at my office along with official crime statistics and a climatology report."

"Best way to tell the weather," he lectured her, "is to step outside."

Go fly a kite, she thought, taking furtive pleasure at her urge to actually say those words to him.

Afterward, as Constance locked the house back up, Stuart Beals cleared his throat officiously.

"Well, the place seems…adequate, although I feel that it's a bit overvalued. Anyway, we have another listing to check out. It's with Arthur Keegan's agency. We'll be in touch."

She said nothing, fighting to keep a straight face. Keegan's so-called real-estate company, located in Antelope Wells clear across the valley, was a holdover from the frontier land-swindle days. Arthur Keegan often appeared in gaudy and loud local TV commercials, wearing a Stetson and a sequined ranch suit, awkwardly twirling a lariat. "Podnahs, lasso your dream home at Artie Keegan's real-estate corral!"

It was easy, this morning, to quickly push all that from her thoughts. She was halfway back to town, the screen of her mind again filling with images from last night, when her cell phone chirred.

Her heart jumped, for any call right now could mean trouble. Or Hazel with a plan of action. Even though her own chief contribution to the day had been to immerse herself in erotic fantasies.

"Hello?"

"It's me, Connie."

"Hazel, hi. Have you run your traps?"

"Did my best. I think I can help you get Quinn to Billings. But I have to admit, this manhunt is heap big doings. Eluding all of it will not be a trip to Santa's lap."

Constance felt her mouth go dry as cotton. So even Hazel could not control the unfolding drama. *I could be in some serious legal trouble*, she realized. *Maybe I will lose my Realtor's license....*

"Connie? Still there?"

"Yes," she managed to say.

"I think I know how you can get around the main roadblock where Highway 17 leaves Mystery Valley. After that, though, you two will be on your own."

Now that the time had arrived for action, Constance felt fear tighten her scalp. "Maybe this isn't such a brilliant idea, Hazel. Maybe—"

"They always talk who never think," Hazel cut her off impatiently. "What, would you rather just throw Quinn to the wolves?"

"Of course not, it's just...I'm scared, Hazel. It's so risky."

"Honey, *life* is a risk. If you believe all the nervous Nellies out there, we'd all live forever if we could just avoid this risk or that. But most of their whining is fraidy-cat hogwash. Ultimately, the death rate is always one per person, risks or no risks.''

Constance laughed. "You're a cracker-barrel philosopher, Hazel, and a good one. You're right.''

"I usually am,'' Hazel reminded her without a trace of modesty. "Connie, I don't want you to be stupid. But don't be afraid to take a worthwhile risk. You do believe Quinn, right?''

She hesitated before answering, unable to shake her memory of that trouble glint in his eyes. Nonetheless, she still had faith in his innocence.

"Yes,'' she finally replied.

"Nuff said. I'll meet with both of you at your place later. Is your house being watched?''

"I'm not sure.''

"We'll assume it is,'' Hazel decided. "It's just a chance we'll have to take.''

"I don't want you to take any of the chances, Hazel. This isn't your problem—''

The old woman cut her off in her gruff fashion. "This involves Mystery, Connie Adams, so it sure as hell is my problem. So I'll explain my plan when I see you. Meantime, you be careful.''

Connie felt the words tight in her throat. "You be careful too, Hazel.''

Chapter 11

As promised, Hazel showed up a few hours after their phone conversation. She gave Quinn Loudon a frank, appraising once-over while Constance took her coat from her and hung it in the hallway closet.

"Quinn," Hazel confided in a low voice, "I admit I don't think very much of your profession—or some in it, anyhow."

"You'll have to do better than that to insult me," he assured her. "I've already come to that same conclusion myself."

Hazel nodded, as if his response confirmed her every instinct about him.

"But that aside," she went on, "I don't care two jackstraws what the news is saying about you. Connie says it's all sheep dip, so I do, too. You're brash and reckless, maybe, but the rest of this is basically lawyers eating lawyers."

Quinn could only smile at the old dame's manner.

Just as Connie had told him, she was immediately reigning over everything with matrician authority.

"It's sheep dip, all right, Mrs. Mc—"

"Hazel."

"Hazel. Thanks for the vote of confidence."

He edged up to the wide front window and glanced outside. The only vehicles in sight were the rental car and Hazel's cinnamon-and-black Fleetwood.

"No one seems to be watching me," Hazel told him as Constance returned to the living room. "Not yet, anyway. I'm not so sure about my place, though."

"You've seen someone?" Constance asked as the two women settled on the sofa.

Quinn stayed in the shadows near the window, listening to them while watching the last daylight fade. It had been gray and gusty all day, the temperature never climbing out of the thirties.

"I haven't," Hazel replied. "But I've told my hands to keep a good watch around the place. Steve Kitchens, he's one of my wranglers, has been breaking some green horses up near the house these past few days. He's noticed a brand-new SUV cruise past the Lazy M several times. It's a Ford, all silver."

Hazel paused a moment to emphasize her next point. "We get the occasional tourists, of course, and they're welcome to stop and take pictures. Hell, sometimes I yak their ears off for 'em. But Steve says these fellows don't look like tourists. One of 'em has plenty of old scar tissue around his eyes—the sign of a bare-knuckles brawler, Steve says, and that young scamp should know—he's got plenty of it, too."

Constance turned troubled eyes toward Quinn.

"Like I said," he told her matter-of-factly, "men

like Roger Ulrick and Dolph Merriday hire out their dirty work. All the more reason why you should bail out, Connie, and let me go it alone from here."

"All the more reason," she corrected him firmly, "that *we* get you to Billings so you can get whatever it is you need to clear up this mess and make the real bad guys go to jail."

That was all Hazel needed to hear. When Quinn tried again to argue it was too dangerous, Hazel used her status as elder matron to simply speak over him.

"My first plan," she informed them, "was simply to drive Quinn myself. But the weather man has scotched that. Why, thank you, dear."

Constance poured her visitor a cup of coffee from a carafe on the glass-topped table in front of the sofa. She'd made it strong and served it black, for Hazel liked her coffee "strong enough to float a horseshoe."

"Weather advisories are posted for the front slopes," Hazel resumed. "Bad snow and ice storms over the foothills and plains east of the mountains. One thing I can't handle so well anymore is a two-ton Cadillac on icy roads."

She leveled her shrewd gaze on Constance. "But you, young lady, can drive like I used to—a little dare-devil when you want to be."

"I'll take on some bad weather," Constance assured her. "But the problem is getting past the road-blocks. And even if I'm not followed, all the authorities are alerted to the rental car."

"You won't be in the rental car. If a car would do it, I'd just let you take mine. But you'll be in your Jeep, which you'll need for my plan."

Even Quinn turned away from the window to stare at Hazel, brows arched in curiosity.

"My Jeep's been seized," Constance reminded her. "It's crime-scene evidence."

"Not really," Hazel said coyly. "Quinn, you're the legal-eagle, you tell her."

Constance saw him smile when he caught on to her meaning.

He looked much better now, she noticed, though pale and drawn from incessant worry and danger.

"Your Jeep," he explained, "was not part of any crime scene. You aren't wanted for anything, I am. The law has a right to hold it because it was used in criminal flight, but only for forty-eight hours for a crime-lab sweep. Sounds like *you're* the legal-eagle, Hazel."

"Shoo, I didn't know about that law until I called a certain...friend in the legal tribe."

"But the Jeep's in Billings," Constance pointed out.

"Not anymore. Right now it's parked in the hay barn behind my house. The gas tank is full, and so is the jerrycan on the bumper. I sent a couple of my hands to Billings last night to drive it back."

"But—won't authorities be watching for the Jeep again, too?" Constance wondered.

A sly twinkle appeared in Hazel's Prussian-blue gaze. "Eventually, sure. But I reached a certain sporting understanding with that friend I mentioned. It will be another twenty-four hours before the computers know the Jeep was released. After that, the law could be all over you two like cheap perfume."

"Twenty-four hours," Quinn repeated. "It could be done, all right, if that bad weather isn't *too* bad. And if we can get the Jeep around the initial road-block."

"That's covered, too," Hazel told him confidently.

She glanced outside. "Good, it's getting dark now. Quinn, how spry are you feeling?"

"Spry enough," he assured her, "thanks to Nurse Connie. What's your plan?"

A youthful deviltry sparked in Hazel's eyes, and suddenly Constance understood how much her friend was enjoying all this. And come to think on it, Hazel *never* shied away from driving in bad weather!

"I unlocked the rear doors of my car before I got out," Hazel informed him. "We're going to count on darkness. You'll sneak out the back right now and go around the corner of the house to my car. Jump in the back and stay down on the floor."

She turned to look at Constance.

"Honey, remember when you and your brother Dwayne were younger, how you used to ask me if you could use the old Summer Trail to ride up into the mountains?"

Constance nodded. Dwayne was twenty-four now, a graduate student in geology at the University of Colorado, Boulder. He was still a full-fledged biking enthusiast, while she had tapered off as her business grew. The Summer Trail led from the pastures near the Lazy M up to the high-country pastures and line shacks. It was seldom used now by cowboys and had long since become the valley's best mountain-bike trail in summer weather.

"The helicopter is grounded tonight because of wind gusts. There'll be a full moon," Hazel hurried on efficiently. "I checked the almanac. Of course there will be clouds, too, so you'll have to drive carefully. But you should be able to follow the Summer Trail without using your lights. That'll get you out of the valley. You can connect with secondary roads to get across the mountains and on to Billings. Are you up to all this, hon?''

Connie nodded, afraid that her voice would give away her inner fear.

"That's the girl! I'll get Quinn into the hay barn where the Jeep is. You wait a half hour after I leave, then drive to my place. Make sure you dress warm. I've talked to some of my boys, and we've got a little diversion planned. When you hear all hell break loose up by the house, that'll be your signal to skedaddle. Just drive right out the back of the barn and follow that rock line fence between my land and Eric Rousseaux's property. It turns into the Summer Trail.''

Hazel stood up, and Constance followed suit. Both women went to the hall closet together to retrieve Hazel's coat.

"You'll have to move quick to beat this bad weather blowing in," Hazel warned her. "You'll be okay once you make the interstate. But even in the Jeep, *don't* get trapped up there in the high country in winter.''

No doubt her fears were betrayed in her eyes, Constance thought, for Hazel gave her an encouraging hug—and Hazel wasn't the "huggy" type.

"Connie, I know I was wrong once. We both were. But I think this Quinn Loudon is a keeper. I really do, and deep down, so do you. I know all we're doing looks bad, but public perception be damned. Do what you believe is right, and risk the consequences.''

"Well," Connie answered with a grim twist to her lips, "you know how the saying goes—fool me once, shame on you, fool me twice, shame on me.''

Hazel hugged her again.

Connie fought unwelcome tears.

* * *

Constance hated waiting. She spent the next half hour pacing and worrying while the twenty-four-hour news channel hummed steadily with the latest NASA goof. Now and then wind whipped up to a bluster and rattled the windowpanes. It seemed an omen, the cold and the snow, but she refused to dwell on it. She'd thrown her lot in with helping Quinn. There was no turning back.

She used part of the time to change into denim jeans and a thick cable-knit sweater. She selected her fur-lined sherpa jacket and warm gloves flexible enough to let her drive in rough terrain.

She ventured into the living room, her eyes glancing at the clock. But then a familiar name blared in the background of the TV.

"...Anders's bullet-ridden body was retrieved from the gravel pit just before dawn today. Dolph Merriday, the prosecutor in the Loudon case, stated earlier he believes Quinn Loudon a likely suspect in the murder of Sheriff Anders. Now for the real story—the weather..."

Stunned, Constance stared blindly at the television. Long minutes passed. Loudon had mentioned Cody Anders. Sheriff Anders could clear him. Now the man was dead. And Quinn the prime suspect.

Lowering her head to her shaking hands, she took stock of herself and the situation. If Loudon had killed Anders, there was no point in mentioning he could clear him. That point, along with Ulrick's nasty surveillance, was still enough for her to believe in Quinn. Her very soul believed him also. But that soul had been duped before by handsome smiles and earnest stories.

But Doug wouldn't have died if she'd withdrawn her belief in him.

Quinn Loudon would surely perish if she abandoned him now.

She stood and turned off the TV.

There was no point in wallowing in her worries and anxiety. Hazel told her to follow her heart. The man who'd made such tender love to her last night was no con artist and certainly no killer.

She grabbed her coat and car keys. There was no turning back from fate and destiny. She believed Quinn Loudon. Hazel even believed him.

And this time, if she must put her own life on the line to prove he was the good person she believed him to be, then she would do it. Do it or perish. From a bullet or a broken heart, she didn't know which.

Yet.

Exactly thirty minutes after Hazel and Quinn left, Constance turned the thermostat down, locked up the house, and went outside to the rental car.

She spotted no one in the early evening gloom and chill. But once on the road to the Lazy M, headlights appeared in the rearview mirror. They stayed far enough behind her to raise doubts but prove nothing.

The vehicle either stopped or turned off when she swung into the driveway of the Lazy M. She saw that Hazel had parked way out back in front of the hay barn—obviously to make it easier for Quinn to sneak into the barn unobserved.

Fighting off nervous jitters, she parked right under the powerful halogen yardlight. She was clearly illuminated as she crossed to the front door and pressed the nacre bellpush.

Hazel's housekeeper, Donna, immediately escorted her through the huge double parlors of the old ranch house, on through to the utility room at the rear of the house.

Hazel was waiting there for her.

"Anybody who might be watching this place from the road," Hazel told her after Donna left, "can't see this part of the yard. Stay behind that line of evergreen shrubs, hon, and go straight to the barn. Remember, wait for the diversion out front, then kick spurs to that Jeep. Good luck!"

Feeling like a character in an espionage movie, Constance ran through the shadows to the big, looming barn. She cast a glance eastward. In the pale moonglow she watched the rapid onsweep of dark clouds. They clustered over the nearby mountains like black rocks piling up.

"Quinn?" she called uncertainly in a low voice after she stepped inside.

"Quinn, where *are* you?"

It was shadowy and dark, but she could see her Jeep parked at the far end of the barn. It faced the open rear doors, all ready to go.

"Quinn? Where are you?"

For a moment, dark panic gripped her like an icy hand squeezing her heart. My God, maybe they'd grabbed him already. Maybe he was even—even dead already, and now they were waiting for her.

Suddenly the barn became a huge, hungry maw waiting to swallow her up. She was on the verge of turning around and bolting. Only abject fear held her in place.

"Quinn! Dammit, Quinn, are you here?"

"Loudon's bolted, lady," rasped a sinister voice behind her, "so you're next."

She cried out, nearly fainting. A hand covered her mouth, another turned her around forcibly.

"Gotcha!"

Almost instantly, she traded her fear for angry indignation. She almost slapped him. "How can you fool around at a time like this?"

"Hey, what better time than now? I need a good laugh. So do you."

"You need a laugh… My God, I almost had a heart attack! It's still thumping!"

He pressed his hand intimately to her sweater front. "Hey, that's good for you, It's like flooring a car to blow out the carbon."

"That's stupid, and so was your prank."

"You're right. It was just something a little nuts to break the tension."

She looked at him. "This will help—they found Anders's body."

He took the news in stunned silence. In his expression, she thought she saw a strange mixture of sadness and relief, but she couldn't tell for sure. All she did know was that the judgment day was now rushing towards them.

"Come on."

He picked up a metal flask wrapped in canvas. He also showed her a Tupperware container.

"Provisions for the outlaw trail, from Hazel. Homemade plum brandy and roast-beef sandwiches. Hazel warned the brandy is just for sipping when we're cold."

"I've had Hazel's plum brandy before," she confided. "If we need it, believe me, it'll also run the Jeep."

He chuckled, and nervousness made her wish she could say something else clever and light. But nothing occurred to her. Fear made her go serious and brooding. Even the mention of brandy made her wonder about her judgment. The need she felt to believe in men—it was like an addiction. There were alcoholics, gambling-holics, even sex-aholics...why not trust-aholics? People addicted to being crushed beneath the shoes of another.

"We should get in the Jeep," he suggested. "Hazel wants us to haul the moment we hear the commotion."

Automatically, Constance started to open the driver's door. Then she hesitated, watching Quinn move around the front of the Jeep, heading toward the passenger's side.

She couldn't make out his face in the shadowy old barn, fragrant with the strong odor of hay. And there was absolutely nothing odd about his suggestions.

But just look, a voice within argued, how you practically jump to carry out his every command. Without willing it, Roger Ulrick's remarks about Quinn's ability to "enthrall" women began to nettle her.

Don't be stupid, she upbraided herself. Quinn isn't some Transylvanian count with mesmeric powers.

He opened his door first, and the soft dome light winked on. She saw that Hazel had given him an old denim work coat and a pair of warm gloves.

Oh, we ladies do take care of him, don't we....

"Something wrong?" he called over, watching her watch him. He looked ruggedly handsome in that muted light, but also shadowy and sinister.

She started to get in, then spotted an object on the floor behind her seat.

"What's that?"

"You're a country girl, and you have to ask?"

"I grew up a townie," she informed him. "My dad owns the hardware store on Warren Street. Grandpa Adams started the store during the Depression."

"I'm not sure what locals call it," he said. "Just a hay hook, I think. They use them when they're bailing hay to pick the bales up and toss them on the wagon. Anyway, I noticed you've got a winch and steel cable on the front of your Jeep. We might be able to use the hook if we get stuck up in the mountains."

Good thinking on his part, she conceded.

But the curving steel hook made her shudder as she swung in behind the wheel and buckled her shoulder harness. The name Cody Anders wasn't very far from her subconscious.

"It's getting cold," she complained, back teeth chattering.

"Start the engine and let the heater run. You should let the engine warm up, anyway. The signal comes any time now."

"Is it safe inside a building?" she wondered. "What about carbon monoxide?"

"You kidding? This place is a cathedral, and besides, the doors are open at both ends. Crank it."

Again, all logical enough suggestions. But her doubts made her overly sensitive about his motives. Or maybe it was just his snap-to-it tone.

"I'm not even driving yet," she complained, "and you're already barking orders. Typical male."

"Blame it on our shrivelled chromosome," he retorted lightly, refusing to engage in battle.

A few moments passed in silence, the only sound their breathing and the barn's old joists groaning in the wind.

"Connie?"

"Yes?"

"Ask you something?"

"What?" Her tone was guarded.

"That look on your face when you first saw me wearing the clothes you gave me—obviously this guy was important to you once. Is that still the case?"

"Did I act like he is last night?" She hadn't intended her tone to sound so harsh.

Evidently she succeeded in irking him. "Well, you didn't cry out his name in bed, no."

She slapped at him, only half-playing. It was a clumsy, silent, and silly gesture with gloves on.

When he spoke, she could hear the grin in his tone, "Don't stop there—it's starting to warm up in here."

"Go to hell."

"Yeah! Even warmer."

Another thirty seconds or so ticked by in torturous silence.

"Hell with this," he snapped out abruptly. "We made love just a few hours ago. Why are we acting like two spiteful kids?"

"I don't know," she confessed in a burst of candid misery.

It wasn't clear who moved first, but a heartbeat later he wrapped her in a tight embrace and kissed her with hungry passion. She felt heat flood her entire body as he pressed her even tighter, exciting her, making her body ache for his.

Even as lust threatened to dash the last bastion of her defenses, she became aware of a sobering, nagging thought about earlier, with Stuart and Pamela Beals. That house represented a tidy commission. Yet, she had "faked" the entire presentation, distracted by ardent thoughts of this man she hardly knew. She was no longer the cold professional she thought she'd made herself into.

Torn between desire and doubt, she abruptly pushed him away.

"What is it?" He spoke only with difficulty, his own desire making him almost hoarse.

"I...we can't get so carried away right now. The signal could come anytime."

"Yeah," he managed. "You're right. This isn't a hot date. Sorry."

Another minute ticked by in unbearable silence. He *must* be able to hear my heart pounding, she thought—her pulse exploded in her ears so loudly she feared she'd never hear the planned distraction because of the unplanned ones.

She did hear it, though, and only moments after worrying about it. A vehicle clattered into the driveway out front, then boisterous voices filled the night—some of Hazel's ranch hands, joshing each other as if returning from a good time in town.

Abruptly Constance heard a loud, flapping sound like a gas oven igniting. Fingers of bright orange light suddenly pushed into the barn from outside.

"Hey, the old Dodge is on fire!" somebody yelled. "Quick, boys, get the fire extinguisher from the bunkhouse!"

"Let's go!" Quinn urged her.

Constance keyed the starter, shifted into first, and

shot through the rear doors of the barn even as the racket intensified out front.

"Billings, here we come," Quinn called out.

She concentrated on her driving as she followed the waist-high rock line fence across a vast, open meadow, barely visible in the cloud-mottled moonlight.

One of her last thoughts, as she turned east onto the old Summer Trail, was about the drive from her house to the Lazy M—and those headlights she'd spotted in the mirror.

It grew steadily colder as they ascended higher into the mountains. Soon the heater was blowing full-blast to keep them warm enough.

Constance left the lights off even after the Lazy M, and the valley floor, were well below them. Moonlight remained generous; when clouds interfered, she simply slowed down and relied on her memory of the Summer Trail's serpentine twists and turns.

She concentrated on her driving, yet remained sharply aware of the man riding beside her. The doubts she had experienced, when they were kissing a little while ago, troubled her like a half-remembered dream.

"You're doing a great job of driving," he remarked at one point. "But don't you think you could probably use your lights now?"

"I'd rather not until we're off the western slopes." She told him about the lights behind her on the way to Hazel's. "If somebody glimpsed lights this high, they might figure out what's happening."

At one point, as she downshifted to climb a sharp upgrade, she misjudged the width of the trail; with a heart-sinking lurch, the left rear and front tires dropped into a narrow declivity.

"Oh, great," she groaned, disgusted at herself. "No traction on two wheels. And look how steep this slope is."

A wind gust buffeted the Jeep, and suddenly dark panic washed over her.

"Quinn, my God! It's *freezing* out there, and we're still miles from—"

"Just take it easy," he cut her off, his voice confident. "When I give you the word, I want you to flip the toggle switch and turn the winch on. Then rev the engine good to keep it powered."

He leaned behind her to get the grappling hook. Cold air sliced into her like a knife edge when Quinn got out and clambered up the slope until he found a strong rock spur and secured the hook. He returned to the front of the Jeep and unwound the half-inch steel cable connected to the winch.

"Hit it, Connie!" he called out after attaching the cable to the hook.

She had never once used the winch, had only bought it because her dad talked her into it. But now, as she felt the vehicle lifting back onto the slope, she reminded herself to give her dad a gigantic hug when she saw him.

"Good thinking," she told Quinn when he got back in, shivering from the blustery cold. "From here, though, I better risk the lights."

Snow started falling, lightly at first, then hard enough that she was forced to switch on the wipers. In the green glow of the dashboard lights, she sneaked sideways peeks at Quinn. He had fallen into a pensive silence.

"This evidence you need—" she remarked. "Will you be able to get your hands on it?"

"We should be okay if we...I mean, once we get to Billings. Thank God I don't need to go to my apartment or my office. What I need is on a computer disk being kept in a safe-deposit box at the Mountain States National Bank on Third Street."

He fell silent, her question the start of a whole new line of worrying.

If he was honest with himself, all he really had, at this stage, was an abstract pattern of guilt inferred from financial and phone records.

Beyond that problem, he also had to prove more than the money laundering. He had to prove he had extenuating reasons for his unlawful flight. In other words, he had to prove that he was the intended victim of a rubout, an attempt to kill him to ensure his silence.

Cody Anders was the key there. His disappearance proved a lot. But with Cody's absent silence, Quinn's reason for flight might be hard to prove. His innocence hung on finding Cody Anders's body and the evidence it held.

Until that happened, he was probably screwed.

He glanced over at Connie, her pretty profile illumined by the dash lights.

Guilt set in as he realized at this point she was in almost as much danger as he was. A completely innocent woman leading a perfectly fine life, and he had to barge into it behind a facade of lies and veiled threats of violence.

But he had *needed* her, he still did. He shuddered to think where he would be right now without her. He would either have died of exposure in back of that cabin or been found there and arrested. But now what he felt for her was far deeper than gratitude—he had finally confirmed that when they made love. She was the kind of woman he'd been looking for all his life and never found. A woman of character and strength. A woman who grappled with the issues of right and wrong just like he did, but a woman who was willing to err on the side of right, even if the whole world sided against her.

He stared at her hard, fighting the notion that he was desperate to possess her, desperate to protect her.

She, and she alone, had kept his hopes alive these past few days. But he had no right to make such incredible demands of her. He, the son of criminals— and evidently a chip off the old cell block, judging from his behavior lately. Look how easily he had leaped across the line separating good citizen from criminal.

"Penny for your thoughts," she said, her voice cutting into the silence.

"Hang on to your money," he advised her, lapsing into grim silence once again.

She watched him, admonishing herself—he's *not* thinking about us. He's only worried about the trouble he's in. You have *not* fallen in love with him.

Even the best Realtor, she reminded herself, can't sell castles in the air.

You've simply mistaken your charged emotions, and the danger lately, for deeper feeling. That was dangerous, and she knew it. His need was transient, and she mustn't build a tower of hopes that must inevitably come crashing down.

Quinn's prolonged silence did nothing to allay her fears.

The steady sweep-and-click of the wipers soon formed a rhythm for the chant in his mind:

> Quinn! Quinn!
> He's our man!
> His ma 'n' pa
> Are in the slam!

Chapter 12

Constance had always been ambitious and competitive, but she dreaded performing under strict time urgency. Yet, they now faced it on two scores.

First they had to get down out of the mountains before bad weather locked them in. Even assuming they succeeded, they had only until tomorrow evening before the Jeep would be back on the mind of authorities.

Plenty of time, she assured herself. Even if driving conditions farther east were slow, Billings could be reached in eight or nine hours.

She didn't ask herself, at this point, what would come after they made Billings. She felt like a soldier trying to cross through enemy fire, only searching desperately for the next object to hide behind.

"Looks like we're almost out of the mountains," Quinn remarked, ending a long silence between them.

"I spotted a section of road down below. Looked like good blacktop."

"It's East County Line Road," Constance informed him. "We're out of Mystery Valley now, which means we're also past the first roadblock."

The mass of precipitation had not yet pushed over the mountains, but waited for them as they descended. Snow pelted them with more force, and there was some accumulation, though nothing the Jeep couldn't handle.

"Here," he said, "put this on. I'll steer while you just put it on over your jacket. Not much of a fashion statement, but it's just for now."

"What is it?"

"The Kevlar vest that saved my life in Kalispell. See, that gives it powers as an amulet to ward off harm. It's good luck now."

"Good, then you wear it. I'm already lucky," she told him. "I meet dangerous men and live a life of derring-do."

"Thanks for the compliment, but humor me, okay?"

"Well…I always *have* wanted to wear one of those," she admitted.

"Atta girl. It's a little big for you, but your clothes under it will bulk you out. Here, I'll steer while you put it on."

It was a clumsy operation while driving, but she managed to wriggle into the surprisingly light and flexible vest.

The final stretch of the Summer Trail turned corkscrew, winding through a series of gullies washed red with eroded soil.

"Quinn?"

"Yeah?"

"I didn't need this vest to figure something out by now."

"That being...?"

"Most of the authorities only mean to arrest you, but there's a few persons who want you...."

"More permanently removed," he finished for her cheerfully.

"Yes. So if you were arrested, by honest authorities, I mean, couldn't you still use your evidence in your defense?"

"Possibly, but see, it gets problematic if I'm arrested. Don't forget, even if I'm legitimately busted, say by state troopers, that could still leave both of us high and dry. I'd never be able to bond out after running once. These guys would have no trouble arranging for an 'accident' while I'm rotting in jail. And then what about you?"

His hand cupped the back of her neck, the touch thrilling her and firing a quick surge of physical need.

But the next moment both of them were jostled hard when the Jeep plunged through a hard dip. County Line Road was only about five minutes away now, perhaps another few hundred feet lower.

He went on. "Even if they can snuff me, they'll sweat over what you might know—what you might *say.*"

The implications of his remark made her heart speed up for a few moments. But again she reminded herself—the danger meant nothing to her if Quinn was innocent.

"So the best shot for both of us," he added, "is to get this evidence of mine to an honest judge, establish probable cause for warrants, then get federal marshals to immediately raid the offices and homes of a few key players.''

Snow flew thicker now, and she switched the wipers to high speed. The Jeep began to level out as the slope ended. Two minutes and we'll be on pavement, she rallied herself.

''Exactly who,'' she asked him, ''do you think actually ordered you…maybe even *us* killed? Ulrick?''

''That one's got me treed,'' he admitted. ''Remember, I'm outside their inner circle, excluded from the power elite. It might just be understood among them, with no actual order being given. But I'd say the nod came from Dolph Merriday. Ulrick's a wimp, but Merriday is strong-willed and he's got national political ambitions. A felony prosecution would probably sink his hopes.''

''*Why* are you outside the inner circle?'' she pressed.

''Hey, that wasn't a complaint, just an observation.''

''You're avoiding the question, counselor,'' she teased him. ''Why are you outside the inner circle? By mistake or by choice?''

''Okay, choice, I guess. It's complicated, but I think mainly it starts in college. In legal circles, even more so in high-power politics, there's this huge social divide between men who pledge the 'right' fraternities and those who don't.''

''You didn't, I presume?''

''You kidding? I'm a pariah. I was Phi Beta Kappa—since that's an honors fraternity, it made me too much of a pointy-headed intellectual type.''

No, just too ethical, she thought. Despite all the

crimes she had seen—even helped—him commit, there was an almost boyish integrity to him.

"So you locked horns with the old-boy network, huh?" she asked. "It exists in real estate, too. I'm just lucky Hazel is the big chief in Mystery, she—oh my God, Quinn!"

She already had her right foot covering the brake. She practically stood on it now, halting their forward progress.

Quinn, too saw it clearly in the pale white moonlight. They had just emerged from the thickly wooded lower slope overlooking the snow-blanketed berm of East County Line Road.

Parked on the shoulder, waiting patiently like a cat beside a mouse hole, was a silver Ford SUV.

"They must have spotted us leave the hay barn," she almost wailed. "They somehow figured it out. What do we—"

"Calm down and keep it together. I don't think they've spotted or heard us yet," Quinn said, cutting her off.

His voice stayed calm, but urgent, thus helping her not to panic. "It's too cold, so they're staying in the vehicle with the engine and heater running. Back up, Connie, nice and easy. Go back into the trees."

She shifted the transmission into reverse. But as luck would have it, her nervously trembling left leg made her foot slip off the clutch. The Jeep bucked once, stalled. Caught in a momentary fluster, she made the mistake of depressing the clutch while she restarted the motor.

They rolled forward again, and this time their luck ran out. Perhaps moonlight reflected off the windshield—at any rate, she heard a muffled shout from below, then two shadowy forms tumbled out of the SUV.

"Back, Connie!" Quinn ordered, his tense voice finally showing the pressure. "I mean haul ass in reverse!"

This time she responded expertly. The Jeep chewed up the trail as it flitted back into the trees, safe for the moment.

Almost immediately, however, she realized they were trapped. The snow-powdered trail was too steep to climb, and already they were scraping forward again as the spinning wheels lost the battle with gravity. In moments they would be exposed again.

"You drive just fine," Quinn told her as he suddenly took over, stretching across her to depress the parking brake and halt their forward slide. "But let me face the bullets. It's my turn to drive. Get in back."

"What do you think you—?"

He ignored her protests and released her shoulder harness, practically stuffing her into the back seat.

"Stay down, way down!" he ordered as he swung into the driver's bucket and started revving the engine. She saw him cram the gearshift into first gear.

"Quinn! What are you doing?"

"Hey, why lock the stable door after the horse has been stolen? Hell, they've seen us—now let's show these bad boys we can get in *their* faces, too. Stay down, Connie!"

Whatever the men below were expecting, it wasn't Quinn's next move. He turned on the headlights, flicked them to high beams, then floored the accelerator as he sidestepped the clutch.

Constance felt herself thrown powerfully backward. Then she was being tossed about violently as Quinn deliberately swerved wildly to right and left.

She heard an abrupt hammering of gunfire, several bullets thonking into the Jeep. Despite the danger, and her bone-numbing fear, she peeked up high enough to see that Quinn had aimed the Jeep directly at the two men.

At the very last moment, both men leaped aside. One of the gunmen loosed a bray of rage or pain, she wasn't sure which.

But Quinn wasn't done just yet. Out in the roadway now, he deliberately backed up fast against the left side of the SUV. It was at a precarious angle on the shoulder—one good hit toppled it onto its side.

He shifted again and tore off toward the east as more gunfire erupted behind them. Again Quinn drove in a reckless swerving pattern to minimize the target. She had all she could do to keep from tumbling around like clothes in a dryer.

When she realized they were safe, at least for the time being, she swallowed to find her voice again. Shaking, she climbed up into the passenger's seat beside him, looking anxiously over her shoulder.

"Were you a Hollywood stunt man before law school?"

He flashed her a nervy grin. "No, but my summer job in college was driving a hack in New York City. What I just did back there—in the Big Apple, that's called parallel parking."

She laughed, more amused by his *sang froid* than his joke. Whatever inner demons were shaking his confidence, this man had no lack of physical courage.

"I sure do apologize for the damage to the Jeep,

though," he added. "If the government doesn't pay for the repairs, I will."

"Right now," she confessed, still trembling from their close call, "I couldn't care less about that."

"Good. Because I can tell you for a fact it will be entered into evidence. Those bullet holes will help establish my case that flight was my only alternative."

My God, we're still swimming the moat, and he's already talking like a lawyer, she thought.

Then she noticed it, just left of the rearview mirror: a neat hole in the windshield, with spider lines radiating out from it.

She looked at Quinn in the dim light, then took off her glove and touched his right cheek. Her finger came away wet with blood.

"An angel kissed me, that's all," he joked lightly before she could react. "It burns a little, but the bullet only grazed me. Luck of the Irish, I guess. Hey, relax."

Relax. She very nearly passed out, dizzy and faint as she realized that death had literally brushed by them. In a way, it really was an angel's kiss. But what if she had been driving in his place.... Death, too, was an angel.

Quinn had told her the truth, and this attempt at cold-blooded murder only lent more credence to his story. The last vestige of any doubt about his innocence vanished from her mind.

"We better wise up and take a new route pretty quick," he told her, his eyes cutting often to the rearview mirror. "I don't know how many goons they've sicced on us, but they might call ahead. Tell me when to turn."

"I guess State Route 23," she decided. "A lot of trucks use it even though it's not the most direct route."

"Good. Just tell me when to turn."

"I don't believe this," she said, still light-headed from fear and adrenaline. "They shot at us!"

"Second time they've tried for me. No, leave that on," he said when she started to slide the Kevlar vest off. "No telling when our trigger-happy friends might drop in again."

Mile after mile rolled past in monotonous safety. Quinn drove now, and Constance welcomed every blessed moment of the monotony.

State Highway 23 was passable, but blowing snow reduced visibility. The steady sweep-and-thump of the wipers was pleasantly hypnotic. Despite the danger they faced, she could not quell the images and sensations she experienced when Quinn's naked flesh had melded with hers.

Sleep remained out of the question. But gradually her tense muscles relaxed again, and she stopped holding her breath every time lights approached the rearview mirror. Twice she turned on the radio to catch state news. But the Quinn Loudon story wasn't even mentioned.

With plenty of heat flowing through the Jeep, she had already removed her sherpa jacket and put it in the back seat. Quinn saw her fussing with the Kevlar vest.

"Know what? Now that we're in traffic, you should put that on under your sweater, not over it. We might be seen by one of the drivers next to us. The vest is pretty distinctive. Might call unnecessary attention to us.''

''But it's huge on me.''

''Won't matter if you're not moving a lot. If somebody spots you wearing it, it doesn't exactly enhance our status as an innocent, all-American couple.''

''What, put it on under my sweater right now?''

''Why not. It's dark. No traffic is close right now.''

''You're close.''

''That's a problem?''

His tone was teasing and daring all at once—and she wondered if it wasn't just her safety that had inspired his suggestion.

''No problem at all,'' she retorted, her tone matching his.

She slid the vest over her head and put it on the floor. Then she grabbed the bottom of her cableknit sweater and tugged the garment off.

He glanced at her with wanting in his eyes before looking back at the road.

Heat stirred inside her, flaring up quick like a match.

''We *can't* stop for a room,'' he said, echoing her own thoughts. ''The clock is ticking. We've got to make Billings.''

''Yes,'' she chimed in, matching the resolve in his voice. ''Billings. A room would be out of the question.''

She slid the vest on, then her sweater. The Jeep entered a long curve where the highway circumvented a big shoulder of granite. Not until they cleared the shoulder, when it was too late to stop without being seen, did they spot the flashing blue lights of the Montana State Troopers.

* * *

"Ride it till it crashes," Quinn muttered.

Constance froze for a few moments, forgetting to breathe.

"Hey, it's not a roadblock," Quinn pointed out as he downshifted and tapped the brakes, slowing down. "Steady, lady, and we'll bluff it."

Sparking flares showed where the left lane had been blocked off ahead. But in the darkness and blowing snow, she couldn't see around the next curve.

"Oh, my God," she muttered. "That bullet hole in the windshield! What if he sees it?"

"Too late now, here he comes. Give him a nice, law-abiding smile, Connie. Come on—that's it, charm the authority out of him."

Quinn rolled down his window, and she felt cold air lick at her. A state trooper built like a granite block stepped closer and thumbed his Smoky Bear hat back.

"Got a jackknifed 18-wheeler up just ahead, folks," he called out, eyes squinted almost shut against the blowing sleet and snow. "Slow way down and go around it in the break-down lane."

"Thanks, officer, we sure will."

Quinn started to roll the window back up. But suddenly the cop turned back toward them, approaching Quinn's window again. Constance felt her heart turn over.

"Gonna be a long delay up ahead at Thompson's Canyon Pass until daylight," he warned them in a friendly voice. "I'd get off the highway for the night. Just a tip."

"Another accident?"

He nodded and began flagging down the car behind

them. He just shrugged before turning to the other driver.

"Either he's just not telling us the reason for the delay," Quinn speculated, "or maybe he doesn't know. That's possible if the FBI has set up a search point."

"What if it's a trick?" Constance suggested. "You know, they lay in wait at the next exit. See who takes the bait and turns off?"

"Yeah, you're thinking like a gangbuster now. Damn! You know another route to Billings?"

"Off the top of my head, just this one and the Interstate. We could look at the map and work out some route by secondary roads. But they won't be plowed yet. And anyway, we'd still have to either pass that checkpoint at Thompson's Canyon Pass or turn off at the only exit between here and there."

"He said until daylight," Quinn pointed out. "If he was telling the truth, that's maybe four hours from now. How far ahead is this pass?"

"Umm, maybe fifteen miles. If I remember correctly the last exit is about five miles before Thompson's Canyon. It's just a little crossroads place called Overland Station. I got water for my radiator there once."

"Any motels there?"

She glanced over at him, but his face was inscrutable in the semidarkness. "I'm not sure. I'd guess so."

"I don't like the idea of any delay. Still—what's your hunch on the trooper? I think he was being straight with us. Feds tend to push them around and insult them. I think he resents them, and they didn't clue the state troopers in. It's crappy duty on a crappy night, etcetera.''

''I don't know,'' she told him honestly, miserable in her indecision. She was scared, and it was hard to choose an option that wasn't dangerous.

''I know it's risky to lay over. But we'll never run that search point. Even with a four-hour stop at Overland Station, we could still make it to Billings in time, right?''

''If the weather doesn't get worse than this, yes. Easily.''

''All right. That's two votes for a motel room.''

It wasn't really, but she said nothing. Despite the pyrotechnics his look had caused her only minutes earlier, she suddenly felt self-conscious, even apprehensive, about the idea of sharing a motel room with Quinn. Even so, her objections weren't enough to overcome her indecision. If she refused, that meant coming up with a better plan.

It wasn't his guilt or innocence she cared about right now, nor even his basic honesty and character. It was herself, her vulnerability and need. She did not want to make the terrible mistake of falling in love with this man. And one more passionate interlude in his arms might be too much to resist.

No, they were not exactly ''two ships that passed in the night.'' But one way or another, the time would come when Quinn Loudon no longer needed her help. She had already survived one hell when Doug left her life; she would *not* place her heart in danger again.

Judging from his next comment, he must have sensed the direction of her thoughts.

''We'll have a long drive ahead of us, and we've both been through plenty lately thanks to my screwups. What say we put in for an early wake-up call and get some sleep? In separate beds,'' he added pointedly, heading off any objections.

''I second your plan,'' she agreed, grateful for his insight. And a good feeling suddenly came over her—the feeling that she was resisting temptation, being responsible and mature.

It's about time I started listening to my head, she congratulated herself.

She had come dangerously close to the precipice; now there was no choice but to leap into the scary unknown or pull back to safety.

Overland Station had sprung up in the nineteenth century when a wagonload of disgusted pioneers gave up on their journey to Oregon and settled right where the axle had busted for the last damn time. Or so claimed a sign of dubious origin in the lobby of the hamlet's only motel, the Cheyenne Lodge.

Quinn's face had been on TV too much lately, so Constance took care of the registration while he waited in the Jeep.

It was past midnight, but someone was watching television behind the front counter when she entered. A middle-aged man with silver hair in a ponytail rose when she entered.

''Howdy,'' he greeted her, flashing a sleepy smile. ''My crystal ball tells me you need a room.''

Her gaze swept the lobby in an all-encompassing pass. Not only were the Ikebana trees in wooden tubs fake, but they didn't exactly complement the buffalo-hide shields hanging on the walls. More like the Cheyenne-Shogun Lodge.

''Actually, two rooms, if possible. Two singles?''

He winced, checking the register. "Two rooms? No can do. You caught me at a bad time, ma'am. Quite a few truckers have taken rooms to avoid a big road-block up ahead."

That was good news, at least, she thought. The trooper was telling the truth.

"'Fraid the best I can do is one double. All I've got left."

She hesitated, and he seemed to read something in her manner.

"We save that room for parents with a child," he confided. "So there's two beds in the room—double and a single."

"I'll take it," she told him, flushing slightly at his curious scrutiny of her.

She handed him the cash, unwilling to use a trace-able charge card. Then took her key and a remote for the TV from him and went back out to the crowded parking lot.

"Only one room left," she told Quinn as she got in. "But there's two beds."

"Oh, praise the Lord," he said with mild irony. "What number?"

"Sixteen—over there at the end."

"That's a good spot. Plenty of trucks will block us from the road."

Quinn maneuvered through all the big rigs choking the lot. When they got out, he took a minute to walk around the Jeep, inspecting it.

The light, at this end of the building, was dim. But Constance saw how the rear bumper had twisted from the impact of pushing the SUV into the ditch.

"You know what?" he told her, gazing at the dam-aged vehicle. "I came out west to do a good job,

make a name for myself in the Justice Department.''
He gave her a self-deprecating grin. ''Man, I sure did
a bang-up job of it. Literally bang-up, if your Jeep is
any proof.''

Even in despondency, his face remained ruggedly
handsome. She could just make out the faint line
where the bullet had creased his cheek. Thinking how
close that bullet came, her arms tingled and she felt
what her mom called a ''truth goose.''

''That vehicle rolled off an assembly line,'' she
reminded him. ''It can be repaired or replaced. You
have my blessing for the damage you did—your dem-
olition-derby driving saved our butts.''

''I *was* pretty damn cool, wasn't I?'' he boasted
playfully as they approached the door of their room.
''I'd say the word 'unflappable' comes to mind.''

''I was duly impressed,'' she assured him. ''Joke
all you want.''

She keyed the worn-out lock and had to play with
it a little before the door swung open. The first thing
she noticed, after she switched on the lights, was the
brightly feathered object suspended from string over
the double bed.

Quinn, peeling off his coat, stepped closer to ex-
amine the light hoop made of ash. It was strung with
catgut webbing and adorned with brightly dyed feath-
ers. ''Too light to be a lacrosse racket,'' he said.
''What in the world is it?''

''You *are* an eastern greenhorn,'' she teased him,
stepping closer to look at it with him. ''Haven't you
ever seen a Native American dream-catcher? It's only
one of the biggest souvenirs in the state. You hang it
over your bed so you can catch your life's secret
dream and make it real.''

Their eyes locked. She was suddenly very aware of his proximity, only inches away. Desire stirred within her like a hungry beast coming awake. She almost expected a spark to arc between them.

"Well, but what if you have a nightmare?" he demanded. "Does it catch that, too, and then make it real?"

"No way. That's the beauty of it, m'love." She tapped the webbing. "It catches dreams, see, but it *blocks* nightmares."

"Talented little doohickey, isn't it?"

"Mm-hmm. Quite."

By now less than three fingers' width separated their lips. She could feel heat literally radiating from him.

"Hey," he said, looking closely at her right cheek.

"Hey what?"

"There's something on your face," he informed her in a hushed voice.

"What?"

"A kiss," he replied even as his mouth met hers.

She lost all sense of time or place as their hungry mouths tasted each other's deliciously burning kisses. Warmth flared within her, and she felt his muscular arms press her even closer, as if he were trying to merge with her.

By some effort of will, however, she tore free from his arms and backed away, putting the double bed between them.

"Bad idea," she reminded him. "We've got four hours until daylight and that roadblock comes down, remember? We have to sleep, then get to Billings."

He still breathed heavily from their searing kisses.

"To hell with sleep. You want the same thing I want."

"Wanting isn't the issue," she assured him.

"No? So what is?"

That, she realized, was the six-million dollar question. But she didn't have the courage to answer it frankly, to tell him flat out that *love* was the issue. Despite the pop tune that claimed otherwise, love had everything to do with it. Everything in the world.

One more bout of pleasure in this man's arms, and she knew she'd be hopelessly gone on him. She *had* to protect herself, knowing her own vulnerabilities. Quinn's need was only masculine lust and his temporary dependence on her. And she had already sensed some terrible struggle going on inside him, some inner tension only he could resolve.

"What is it?" he demanded again, baffled by her long silence, and impatient too.

"Let's just say," she suggested in a dismissive tone, "that it's more than a quibble, but less than a quarrel, okay?"

Despite his frustration, he couldn't help laughing at the way she wriggled out of answering him.

"Nice sidestepping. Who's the lawyer here, lady? That's some mighty impressive verbal hair-splitting."

Constance was headed toward the bathroom. "First dibs on the shower."

"Can I hold the soap for you?" he called out behind her.

"Nuh-uh. And I'll use up all the hot water," she promised him. "Obviously, cold water is what you need, counselor."

Chapter 13

Despite teasing Quinn, it was she who took the first cold shower in a futile attempt to quell her desires. All it really accomplished, however, was to make her recall even more hungrily the heat of his body, his hot, solid masculinity touching her inside and out.

The bathroom was cold and drafty, with burned-out bulbs in the heat lamp. But it was clean and there were plenty of thick white towels. A big bath towel became her wrap-around nightie.

"All yours," she told him as she came out into the cozy warmth of the room, still combing out her wet hair.

"Tempting words." He sat on the single bed, removing his shoes. His eyes caressed the length of her body.

"I meant the *bathroom* is all yours," she corrected herself. "And I even left you some hot water."

But he made no effort to move, still watching her. "Connie?"

"Yes?" She paused halfway to her bed, watching him with expectant, curious eyes.

"Look, ahmm…we both made up our minds to…*sleep* while we're here, right? No fooling around."

Warily she watched him. "Yes?"

"That being the case, I have a request."

"A…request?"

"Yeah, sort of a noncontact consolation prize."

"And that would be…?"

Strong white teeth flashed at her when he grinned. "That would be you dropping your towel for a minute so I can get a good eyeful of you bare naked."

She sent him a suspicious look, her skeptical dimple appearing.

"Just one good look at you in the buff," he cajoled. "Look, I'll stay right here on the bed. Scout's honor. No attempts to touch you."

A strange thrill slid down her spine. Actually, the idea rattled her, because it wasn't his will she was worried about. She wanted to look into his eyes and feel his desire for her.

But she didn't trust herself to stop, to resist once their little "game" got started.

"What's the big deal?" he persisted. "We're not exactly strangers, you know."

The "big deal," she thought, but couldn't find words to say, was her fear of falling in love with him. Sure, the mechanics of sex were no big deal, that part was easy. Anyone could take pleasure when it was offered. But how would she fill the hole in her heart after Quinn stopped needing her help—when he was gone from her life, and yet she needed him like she needed breath in her nostrils?

"Just a feast for my eyes," he implored, "and then I'll go take that cold shower. One peek to stoke my dreams."

"I don't trust you," she demurred. "This is a clever ruse to seduce me."

"A ruse? Are you saying that seeing a woman naked—a woman like you, anyway—isn't its own reward? C'mon, shuck that damn towel, girl."

She hesitated, self-conscious. The room was dark except for the light spilling out behind her from the steamy bathroom.

Seeing her debate inwardly, a sly smile tugged at his lips. One more little nudge, that smile said, and she'll do it.

"Connie, think about this. Our sun, and all the rest of the stars, *must* die when they consume the last of the fuel at their cores. Nobody can stop it, not even Bill Gates. All of civilization is doomed. So you please tell me—what's the big deal about letting me see you naked?"

They both smiled at his cosmic sophistry.

"Quinn Loudon," she retorted in a mock Irish accent, "you've kissed the Blarney Stone, all right. But I like it."

Even as she spoke, he grabbed the towel. By instinct she tugged it back to her but he pulled it to the carpet.

The mirth left his face, and she saw him swallow with difficulty as his eyes drank in the sight.

Feeling bolder than she'd expected, she simply stood before him, fighting the urge to cover herself with her hands.

"Yeah, I see now why you're so drawn to painting," he said in a throaty husk after looking at her for a long moment in silence. "You're a work of art yourself."

She scooped up the towel and wrapped it around herself again.

"Nice try," she teased him, trying desperately not to get caught up and needful of his admiration, "but you can't charm me into bed. To quote Hazel, you're jabbering pure piffle. Hit the shower, sport."

"It is pretty late, isn't it?" he said reluctantly, heading for the bathroom.

"Speaking of which, did you request a wake-up call?"

"I forgot, but don't worry," she assured him. "I've got this infallible inner alarm clock. I wake up right after sunrise no matter how little I've slept."

While Quinn took a shower she used the room phone to take care of another detail she'd forgotten. She dialled the number at her real-estate office and waited for the answering machine to click on.

"Ginny, hi, it's me. It's early Wednesday morning. I'm going to miss at least another day of work. I'm fine, okay? I promise to explain all of this as soon as I can. And I have to ask a big favor of you—find some way to downplay all this for my mother when she calls the office? You two get along well, just assure her that I'm okay. Later, kiddo."

She was in bed, covers tucked under her chin, when Quinn emerged from the bathroom.

"Do I at least get a merit badge for this?" he grumped as he climbed alone into the bed on the other side of the room.

"Whatever doesn't kill you can only make you

stronger,'' she teased, surprised at how quickly she was becoming drowsy. It was all that danger and excitement when they were shot at, she realized—stress was taking its toll.

''Quinn?'' Her tone was serious now.

''Yeah?''

''I know you don't want me to know too much. But…who can you trust once you get that computer disk? I mean, who will you give it to? Your lawyer?''

''I've been wrestling with that one. Not my lawyer. Lance Pollard will almost surely be under observation. I think Mumford is our boy.''

''Todd Mumford? The FBI agent who was with Ulrick the first time he grilled me?''

''Yeah. I trust him, and obviously he's close to the case. Also, by now Todd has probably made some observations on his own. He's sharp.''

''Observations? Like what?''

''Sometimes little strokes fell great oaks. By now these guys have left a trail of little clues in their illegal attempts to snuff us out, and Todd must have noticed something. Don't forget I've got two separate but related cases to prove—the kickback conspiracy and the subsequent attempt on our lives.''

''Will you…I mean, are you going to surrender to him, too?''

''I think I'll have to, Connie. I might be able to prove an extenuating case for flight. But not if I keep it up indefinitely. Do you realize we're starting the sixth day of this nightmare?''

''Nightmare,'' she repeated, exhaustion slowing down her speech. ''If that's what's happening, then I wish at least one of us could wake up from it.''

''Maybe we'd be okay,'' he suggested, ''if we *both*

get under that dream-catcher dangling over your bed? You said it blocks nightmares, remember?''

Even falling asleep, she grinned in the darkness. ''Go to sleep. I have a very short fuse around you, counselor. Stop playing with fire.''

It was not Quinn alone, however, who was eager to play with fire.

Although Constance quickly dozed off, she never really reached the depths of true sleep. She was cold and kept dreaming of warm strong arms. Increasingly erotic dreams kept her physically aroused, restless with pent-up desire.

Again and again she relived the sights and sensations of their lovemaking. Seeing his hard masculine nakedness as he slept at her house, winter moonlight making him gleam like smooth ivory; the surprise of his voice calling her into bed; the fire in her loins as his hands glided under her chemise; the overwhelming, explosive pleasure as he thrust deep into her....

With a whirring click, the room's electric heater kicked on, and she woke up at the noise.

She realized immediately he was still there in the room with her. His breathing was deep and even. Almost peaceful.

She checked the green-glowing face of her watch on the nightstand: only 1:30 a.m. She'd dozed, if that's what the interlude could be called, less than an hour.

She could hear Quinn turning in the bed. She wondered if he was dreaming the same erotic dreams she had.

''Quinn?'' she called softly from her bed. ''Are you awake?''

Silence.

Regretfully, she reminded herself that she was the one who imposed this stupid separate-beds arrangement. Nothing for it now but to tough it out, try to go back to sleep.

She tossed and turned, desperate to get comfortable, but unable to quell the rising storm of her thoughts.

"Can't sleep either?" Quinn's voice suddenly sliced into the silence.

She smiled into the darkness. "I would have thought I'd be exhausted, but it's not working. I just can't let go and relax."

He rolled from his bed and slid into the covers beside her. She wanted to protest, but something stopped her.

Probably the irresistible warmth of his hard naked body.

"I was on the verge of waking you up," he confessed.

"We shouldn't get involved like this, Quinn. It's only going to mean a mess later."

A long silence passed between them as he stared at her in the dark.

Finally, in a harsh voice, he whispered, "I can't promise the end's going to be pretty. But it's later and right now we don't know how much later we have, so…"

As if both of them were of one mind, both wound to the extremes of sexual tension, his mouth found hers and took it in a demanding kiss. He pushed inside her with the next kiss. Her first climax was fast and explosive.

Her natural animal passion for him was magnified

through the lens of danger, and in the charged, heady atmosphere, it seemed neither of them could sate their need. Her legs wrapped around him, her nails pressed into the taut muscles of his back, she cried out over and over in an ecstasy of release.

Outside the room, blowing snow pelted the windows, and the Montana blizzard howled with a haunting shriek like souls in torment.

Inside, however, the two lovers experienced a few hours of blessed oblivion, safe and secure in the private little world of pleasure they made for themselves.

Not until the pale, leaden light of dawn showed in the window did they finally return to the cold reality of their plight.

They were both still awake, though physically exhausted. Constance, feeling lethargic and sated, watched Quinn as he pushed up on one elbow to look at her lying beside him. One finger traced the outline of her profile.

"All night long," she told him softly as he bent to kiss the tissue-thin skin of her eyelids. "Again. And Billings is still calling us."

"Uh-huh. Time to roll out and hit the highway."

"I know."

But a moment later, when neither one of them made any move to get up, they both laughed like silly school kids trying to talk each other into playing hooky.

"You first," she insisted. "Age before beauty."

"No way. You first. Then I get to see you naked again."

She snuggled against him, kissing the matted curls of his chest hair. Right then, the last thing she wanted to do was go outside into the cold winter morning. If only she could just stay here with him like this forever.

"You say that as if this is our last time together," she pointed out.

"Well, how do you know it's not?" he parried, the playfulness gone from his tone now.

Again she rose up to look at him. But he stubbornly avoided her gaze, as if annoyed, all of a sudden, by such close scrutiny.

"Are you that pessimistic about proving your innocence?" she demanded.

"It's not just that," he said evasively.

"Then what?" Her voice was low and hesitant. Fragile.

He just couldn't bring himself to say it. He was convinced, down deep in his heart of hearts, that he wasn't good enough for her.

How *could* he be, he wondered each time he frankly considered his plight. The enormous faith she had shown in him, the risks she had taken—all of it moved him more deeply than he could find words to express.

And yet, that very faith also served to emphasize starkly his own questionable character. Lost in her arms, nothing mattered because thought was banished by the oblivion of pleasure. But after their lust was sated, there was nothing left for them. For try as he might, he couldn't come to grips with the ease of turning criminal to protect himself.

The leopard cannot change its spots....

She waited for him to go on, trying to read the turmoil of his feelings.

"So if it's not just legal troubles on your mind," she pressed him, "what else is it?"

He shook his head, swinging his legs out of bed, then standing up. He combed his hair with his fingers while he tried to come up with something worth saying. With a low groan, he seemed to give up.

"I guess some things just aren't in the cards," was all he said.

He didn't intend it to sound as blunt and cruel as it did to Constance. She sat up, clutching the sheet over her breasts. Anger and hurt shaped her tone.

"You don't waste any time giving a woman the kiss-off. Slam, bam, thank you, ma'am. Are you going to leave some money on the dresser, too? Maybe recommend me to some of your buddies?"

He pulled his clothes on while she talked.

Finally, in exasperation, he turned to her. "You couldn't be more wrong if you were trying," he assured her, his face a study in misery. "Nobody's giving you the kiss-off. Nobody in *this* room, anyway."

"No? Fine, I'm *trying* to understand all this, Quinn! What in the world is wrong?"

"I...it's just that I...oh, Christ, just never mind. Look, you'd better get dressed. I noticed a coffee shop across the road. Let's get a shot of caffeine for the road."

He wanted to say something else; he truly did. But he didn't know how to go about the job of admitting his own fear of inferiority. Feelings didn't always match up well with the words needed to express them.

Yes, she made him happy—deliriously so. He knew by now that he had never loved a woman the way he loved Constance.

That part, if it were all, would be easy enough to

say. But it wasn't all. Not by half. Just then a phrase from the law occurred to him: *acquired by escheat.*

This happiness he felt—it was his by false representation. Even if he could beat the charges drummed up by his enemies, there was a guilty verdict in the jury of his mind.

Constance interpreted his silence as a sullen rejection of her. Feeling self-conscious now about her nakedness, she quickly dressed. The silence in the room first infuriated, then saddened her. They had spent such a rapturous period of love, and now this painful silence, this terrible impediment that she could not even understand.

"You forgot the vest," he reminded her as she pulled her sweater on.

"To hell with the vest," she snapped, tossing it at him. "You wear it. Take care of number one, right?"

"Connie, listen, I—"

"No point in dragging this out, is there?" she cut him off curtly. "Let's get to Billings so you can do your thing. I've got a life on hold right now, and I need to get back to it."

Chapter 14

On Tuesday evening, only minutes after Constance and Quinn escaped out the back of Hazel's hay barn, Steve Kitchens knocked on the door, bearing bad news.

"Hazel," the young horse wrangler informed her, "the truck fire is out. But I don't think the trick worked. Me and Gary saw somebody go hightailing toward the road right after the Jeep left. Whoever it was must've been hiding behind the old pumphouse in the east pasture."

"You can see the whole spread from there," she confirmed, chastising herself for not remembering it before this.

"Anyhow, they lit out before we could get over there. Took off east toward the mountains."

"Was it that same silver SUV?" the rancher pressed.

"None of us could swear to the color or make. But

it sure-God looked like an SUV to me. Gary said so, too."

So the sneaking prairie rats had actually trespassed, Hazel fumed. They had hidden on her property like thieves in the night.

That tears it, she decided. They had pushed it too far, and now she was in this fight, too, whether Connie liked it or not. Time to call in some favors.

After Steve left, bearing orders for an all-night guard, Hazel called the personal number of Governor Collins at his mansion in Helena.

"Caller ID shows a Mystery phone number," a deep, folksy voice greeted her. "That you, Hazel?"

"Just checking up on you, Mike. I know things the voters don't. Things Marsha doesn't know, either."

They both laughed, knowing some of what she said was true, but not enough to worry about.

"How you doing, young lady? Haven't heard from you since you folks invited me down to your sesquicentennial."

"I'm ornery and bullheaded as ever," she assured him. "But we seem to have us a bit of a situation here. You busy?"

"Busy as a moth in a mitten. But so what? Cold day in hell, I can't find time for Montana's favorite daughter."

"Mike, does the name Quinn Loudon ring a bell?"

"Loudon? Are you joking with me? I don't know him personally, but his name's been all over the news lately. Blasted his way out of the courthouse in Kalispell. Assistant U.S. Attorney."

"That's our boy."

"Matter of fact, Hazel, one of my aides has been

keeping me posted on that case. It seems that Loudon is bad medicine.''

''You've got it hindsight foremost,'' she corrected him. ''Some bent lawyers are trying to make him their pigeon.''

The governor's voice lost some of its well-practiced folksiness as he was caught flat-footed by her claim. ''You sure about that?''

''Sure as we're talking. I don't know the whole scheme, no. But let me tell you some things I'm sure your aide doesn't know.''

Quickly and efficiently she brought the governor up to speed concerning the unreported nature of the manhunt for Loudon. She did not register any complaints about accepted legal tactics, such as the routine questioning by Roger Ulrick and Todd Mumford.

Rather, she emphasized those points that did not qualify as legitimate police work in her view. Things like the sacking of the Hupenbecker cabin, causing damage, and all the spying and tailing and trespassing by men who looked like wanted posters, not cops.

Nor was she bashful about fingering Ulrick as a crooked prosecutor. She had promised Connie to squash Ulrick like the roach that he was, and she meant it. To Hazel, plenty of things the law called ''crimes'' didn't bother her much. But those who betrayed their oath of public office were even lower than horsebeaters, and that was going mighty damn low in rural Montana.

Governor Collins listened carefully, growing more and more engrossed in the story. He asked several pertinent questions, and quickly agreed with Hazel that the matter was top priority. Instead of doing her a favor, he made it clear she had done the favor by calling.

"I'm having a telecon with the state attorney general about this as soon as I hang up," he promised. "This goldang highway-construction mess has been a black eye for this state, and my administration, for too long now. This might be the best opportunity yet to nail the key players and finally clean up this mess."

"A new broom sweeps clean," Hazel encouraged him. "Lock 'em up and hire some straight-shooters."

Hazel did not hang up, however, until conveying her heartfelt belief that hired killers were even now stalking Quinn and Connie. Governor Collins promised to alert state troopers about the situation. Since they had no license tag number for the SUV, they'd look for the Jeep instead.

While Hazel was on the telephone, her housekeeper built up a fire in the big fieldstone fireplace. After Hazel hung up, she gazed for a long time at the cheery, crackling flames, feeling ambivalent about what she'd just done.

She decided, again, that she'd had no choice but to call in the governor—her plan to get Connie and Quinn safely to Billings had apparently failed from the get-go. Now Hazel felt responsible for protecting them, even if it meant letting the law pick them up.

She knew she had an obligation to protect them—especially Connie. Hazel's dream of saving Mystery through behind-the-scenes matchmaking had not diminished. Not one blessed whit. Nor had the plain old *fun* of it. But she did not want her machinations to endanger anyone.

Her line of thought naturally prompted her to lift her gaze to the oval, sepia-tone photograph of Jake

McCallum hanging over the fireplace. Her square-bearded, iron-eyed ancestor looked back down at her, just as he might be watching right now from the afterlife.

Jake had always believed that money was like manure—it worked best when you spread it around. By spreading theirs around, successive generations of McCallums helped create the community of Mystery.

But money alone, she told herself, could not ensure the ongoing identity of a place. Only love and commitment could do that. Hazel was convinced that, with certain impediments removed, Connie and Quinn could share a love as deep and abiding as Hazel still felt for her own long-dead husband. And they would raise a wonderful family to help keep Mystery a place where hope prevailed.

Still—those "impediments" had lately gotten very dangerous. Hazel loved Connie like the daughter she never had.

"Lord," she said softly, "I hope I haven't been too clever for Connie's own good. I could have driven Quinn myself, but I had to be sly. Please don't let my fool-headed tricks put those two in harm's way."

As she always did for comfort, she drew aside her lace curtains and stared at the mountains. Her strength. Her sustenance.

Constance could not get a handle on her turbulent emotions as she and Quinn put Overland Station in the rearview mirror at sunup, sipping extra-large cups of mediocre but strong coffee.

Anger made a tight mask of her features, but she wasn't sure at whom it was directed, Quinn or herself. After all, she had predicted this very outcome—that he would pull back from her once he no longer needed her help. And just look. Not until this final stretch to Billings did he hand her that malarkey about how "some things just aren't in the cards."

She had let him drive, and the weather that morning was blue-lip cold but clear and sunny. Several times Quinn tried to engage her in conversation. But each time she either ignored him or responded in short cool clips.

Finally, frustrated by her attitude, Quinn said pointedly, "No need to get your nose out of joint. You act like I deflowered you and then deserted you at the altar."

His barb thrust deep, drawing blood from old wounds. For a few moments she was convinced she positively hated this backsliding creep.

"Know what? You need some serious couch time," she informed him archly. "You could explore some basic issues such as your contempt for women."

The moment she said it, however, she regretted the remark. It was inspired by pique, not her real belief. Despite his behavior last Friday at the cabin, and a little while ago in the motel room, she was convinced—his personal problem was not with women or anyone else.

The handsome swordsman was locked in a deadly struggle with another version of his self. A darker, more cynical and defeatist version that wanted to become his nature versus the strong, hopeful, idealistic self that *was* his real nature. One or the other was on the verge of winning, but she couldn't tell which.

Unfortunately, she was too angry and upset to tell him all that.

Even when she saw how her insult made his knuckles turn white on the steering wheel.

"You know how it is," he replied, his tone flat with suppressed anger, "with those of us who have inherited the criminal gene. That's why I attacked you repeatedly."

"Quinn, I'm sor—"

"Save it for your memoirs," he snapped, obviously still smarting. But his anger shaded over into resentment, and he added, "You know what? I'd kiss the devil's ass in hell if I could change my past. But I can't."

"Quinn, I'm sorry. I didn't mean that the way it sounded, okay? I'm confused and frustrated, and I spoke carelessly."

A moment later, he too relented a bit. "I guess I didn't mean to be so thin-skinned, either. Maybe you scraped a raw nerve."

"Well, yes, you *are* thin-skinned about your past. It means far less to me than you apparently think it does."

His response confirmed her insight from moments ago.

"It's not just you," he told her, his words halting and uneasy. "Actually, it's all me. That's what's so damned frustrating. This thing is self-inflicted. It wouldn't matter what you said, even if I believed you. Not so deep down, Connie, I just can't convince myself I'm good enough for you. For *any* decent woman. I know it sounds stupid, but things are the way they are. And this whole episode from the courthouse to here has cut all my scars wide open."

"Is that what you were trying to say back in the motel?"

He nodded.

"It's completely logical you'd feel that way. But you're just plain *wrong,* Quinn Loudon. You couldn't be more wrong."

Her words, ringing with heartfelt sincerity, moved him so deeply he was forced to silence, afraid he couldn't command his voice. What she just said was typical of the enormous faith she'd shown in him almost from the beginning of this reckless, dangerous adventure.

But none of that mattered.

The best way to help this well-intended woman, he decided, was to make sure she dropped him like a bad habit. He only hoped now that he could finish the damnable drive without getting her into more danger.

He swallowed and said in a tone heavy with unbending finality, "Connie, even if I am wrong, it doesn't matter. You need to find someone who's more like you, who's compatible and supportive and all that stuff. And who's definitely law-abiding."

His tone, and the hard set of his features, lacerated her heart even more than the trite, cruel words. It was definitely the tone of that darker, defeatist self vying to dominate him. But she lacked the courage to say that, to even respond.

This was all so wrong, she despaired, so unfair and even frustratingly tragic, like a crucial tryst that never takes place because a doorbell was broken.

After she caught Doug red-handed, she had sworn no man would get close to her again until he had practically been certified by the Nuclear Regulatory Commission.

Then fate crossed her path with Quinn's. She could fool herself no longer—despite precautions, she had fallen hopelessly in love with him. And she knew that she would gladly forgive him everything, if only he could forgive himself. Somehow she'd have to find the courage to say that, not just think it.

He said something she missed. "What?"

"Not such a good time to be so distracted, Connie. Those goons we stranded could be cruising the highways by now. And now that it's daylight, this dinged-up Jeep will attract police attention."

"You're right," she said, keeping her own tone carefully businesslike.

She did become more vigilant, especially watching carefully in the right side mirror. Obviously, however, Quinn too was still having trouble focusing his thoughts, judging from his next comment.

"There's this other possibility neither one of us has mentioned. We're both assuming I can clear myself. But some very powerful and connected attorneys are trying to ensure otherwise. Guys who make up their own rules. So even if…things could be different between us, it still might not matter. A conviction could lock me away for twenty years."

She could hardly look at him across the car seat. She knew what she would find on his face. The tight expression. The darkness in his eyes. He was right, of course. He could be taken from her for twenty years. Fate could be so cruel. Fate had already been cruel to both of them.

But Constance knew that she would gladly cross that bridge with him when they got to it, if only he'd let her into his life. She'd never let a false conviction stand. Somehow, some way, she'd fight to clear him.

But still none of that mattered.

Because he *wouldn't* let her in. Unless he somehow

squared things with himself, she'd have better luck trying to sell those castles in the air.

So all she said was, "You'll clear yourself. Don't forget Hazel. I could tell she likes you. She'll fight for you."

"I like her, too. She's a real character without trying to work at it. I hope she can help me—with the rap sheet I've accumulated by now, I'll need all the help I can get."

Yes, she thought silently, eyes burning as she willed back tears. We both will.

Chapter 15

Perhaps the wheel of fortune had finally swung their way.

By deliberately staying boxed in between the many big tractor-trailer rigs that used State Route 23, Quinn kept a low highway profile. Constance spotted two police cruisers in the westbound lanes, and each time she braced for trouble. But neither one came charging across the median to arrest them.

They finally reached Billings just before noon. The city looked pretty and pristine under its new powdering of snow. The Mountain States National Bank occupied a pompous red-granite building on Third Street downtown. Quinn circled the block once to check things out.

"Looks like just one rent-a-cop outside the door," he told Connie as he parked across the street half a block away. "Here's hoping he's as dumb as he looks. When I get out you slip behind the wheel, okay? Move on down a little closer in case I come out running. You'll drive from here. What?'' he added when she suddenly surprised him by laughing.

"Us," she said bluntly as he got out. "Everything you just said—sounds like we're robbing the bank."

"Well, that's a good sign, you laughing about it."

"Why?"

"Means you've gone a little nuts. Best way to survive."

She watched his breath forming white wraiths in the chill air.

"Be careful," she said before he shut the door.

"You, too."

Their eyes locked for a long moment, recalling sweeter things than their disagreements.

He reached out and ran his cold hand down her cold cheek. "Whatever comes down from here," he said grimly, "I just want you to know I've never fallen for any woman the way I have for you. Know what you are? Moonlight on the waves—just as beautiful and perfect as that painting at your house. Don't forget that, okay?"

With that he was gone, crisp snow crunching under his feet.

She watched his back retreat, still fighting off tears that stung to be released. She couldn't lose it now, she admonished herself. Quinn's fate depended on her keeping it together.

She swung her door open and stepped outside, instantly refreshed by the bracing slap of the cold winter air. She held her breath as Quinn got a cursory once-over from the security guard. Then Quinn disappeared into the bank, and she released a long sigh of relief.

She went around to the driver's side and got in,

forced to smile when she saw how far back the seat was to accommodate his long legs. Sliding the seat forward, she slowly drove ahead.

She parked three cars back from the doors of the bank and waited, praying no trap lay within to snare Quinn.

However, he emerged perhaps five minutes later, his face jubilant, and she expelled a huge sigh of relief. He slid into the passenger's seat, and she saw the red plastic computer-disk case in his hand.

"So far, so good. Here's the original and a copy," he told her, opening the case to check. "Now comes the hard part—turning myself over to Todd Mumford."

"Shouldn't you call him first?"

"I just did from a pay phone in the bank. He's in his office and knows we're coming."

Alarm widened her eyes. "Will it just be him?"

"That's what he promised, and he's a decent guy. But he's also a cop, so get psyched up for anything—God knows what kind of a reception we're going to get. Turn right on Seventh Avenue and take it six blocks to the Federal Building."

"I guess I've got a lot of explaining to do, too," she murmured, still trying to follow his directions.

He took her hand and squeezed it. There was a new light in his face, and the relief opened his normally closed expression. "My hunch is nothing that will stick. But that all depends how this whole thing shakes out. A prosecutor would have to convince a grand jury to indict you, and that's tough in hostage cases—hostages get every benefit of the doubt, and then some, for what they do."

"I refuse to be a hostage. So what then?"

He shook his head at her stubbornness. "You would," he griped, amused. "But even so, any indictment from a grand jury would be tossed by a jury if I insist I threatened you with harm if you didn't cooperate. I'll just tell them you're lying now out of fear. Now what do you say to that?"

"Nonsense. I won't let you do that, no matter how smart and lawyerly you get. You're innocent, and I'll face the music for what I did. I don't regret one thing—about that," she added, more for herself.

"Yeah, well, that's real noble and all that. But you can just can the self-incriminating stuff right now," he warned. "If you're arrested when we get there, say nothing except where's my lawyer. Remember, it's a long way from an arrest to a conviction."

"I will remember it, and you do the same," she encouraged him as the big Federal Building loomed into view on their right.

It was an impressive structure, nineteenth century and Romanesque, with plenty of rounded arches. A frieze sculpted in bas relief ornamented the outside.

"You'd think we were going to the opera," she remarked.

"Park in the side lot," Quinn instructed her, craning his neck to glance nervously all around them. The plaza out front was crawling with FBI and ATF agents, some in "blackout" jumpsuits and well-armed. But unless it was a good act, he decided, they were clearly not expecting anything special. No media bozos, either.

"Talk about the lion's den," he said as she parked in a free lot south of the building. "Todd said it's best we use the service entrance in the back. He's on the third floor, and there's a stairwell hardly anyone uses but maintenance workers.''

By now Constance felt flutters of nausea. She almost got sick by the time they were halfway up the dingy, unlighted stairs.

Quinn linked arms with her to support her.

''We'll go when you're ready,'' he said gently, his hand on the door to the third-floor hallway.

She gazed into his smoky eyes and saw no fear in them—just determination to see this through.

She nodded. ''Ready.''

From that point on, it was all a blur to Constance. They were in a brightly lighted hallway, its bare walls painted an ugly, impersonal shade like pale mustard. They passed several doors, and then Quinn guided her into a pleasant, wainscoted room. No armed cops, no reporters, no net to snare them—yet.

Just a grinning, baby-faced Todd Mumford, sitting on one corner of his desk looking fresh-scrubbed and precocious. He stood up as they entered.

''Well, if it isn't the *enfant terrible* of law enforcement,'' he greeted Quinn. ''Buddy, you could use a shave. You look rough. Hi, Miss Adams. Have a seat, both of you.''

His eyes flicked to the case in Quinn's hand. ''That money-laundering data you mentioned, right?''

Quinn handed it to him. ''My computer's compatible, so go ahead and boot it up. I've already plotted the graphs and plugged in the variables. You can look at it and trace each bribe payment, from the date it transpires to the final investment shelter. Not just the financial end, but all phone and written transactions to support it. I know it's not everything, but it's a start. It's sure all I have.''

By now Constance had calmed down enough to notice details. Such as the knowing little smile in Todd Mumford's eyes when Quinn made his last comment.

"Oh, this might not be *all* you have," the FBI agent suggested as he slid one of the disks into the personal computer atop his desk. "Matter of fact, Quinn, I'll lay fifty-to-one odds this is merely going to ice a very nice cake for you."

"Lost me on that one," Quinn admitted.

Mumford was barely listening now, absorbed in his computer screen. He loosed a sharp whistle.

"Good work, ace! With this plus everything else we've already got sewn up, my grandmother could prosecute this case."

"Everything else?" Quinn repeated, suddenly starting to catch on that something big was about to happen in his life. "Like what?"

Mumford's eyes, as blue and bright as forget-me-nots, cut to Constance.

She had taken a seat on a ladderback chair, nervous stomach still feeling like she was in a fast elevator.

"I have a message for you from Governor Collins," Mumford informed her.

"For me?" Now she was as confused as Quinn. The young fed was so pleased with himself he couldn't stop grinning. Clearly he wanted to extend the moment. His was the smug, excited, knowing grin of a schoolyard chum who knows something *you* don't know.

"Yes, definitely for you. On behalf of the citizens of the state of Montana, he thanks you for your courage in assisting Quinn Loudon. And—his exact words now—'for God sakes *please* call Hazel and your mother and tell them both you're all right. They're worried sick.'"

Constance looked at Quinn, who still resembled a man waking up from a twenty-year coma.

"Hazel," she told him, and now, as she began to understand, she felt the slight tickle as a tear formed in the corner of her right eye. "Didn't I tell you?"

But something else occurred to her, and she looked at Mumford. "But...what about Quinn?"

"Well, we'll need him to swear out some lengthy and boring depositions. But when we found Sheriff Anders's body, we found a fingerprint on his holster that hooked up to a hit man on Whitaker's dole. It was exactly as Quinn said. Anders's life was in danger along with Quinn's, but no one was ready to listen then. We are now."

He turned to Quinn. The agent stood up from his computer and shook Loudon's hand. "You're a free man, Mr. Loudon."

Quinn closed his eyes, unspeakable relief washing over his face.

But when he opened them again, she saw the darkness back again.

"Could you please tell Cody's wife I'm sorry to hear about her husband. I wish I could have done more to warn him—"

"You didn't know how far this would go, Quinn. Above all, you've proved you're a man of honor. You would have saved Anders if you could."

Mumford's words seemed scant comfort to Quinn, but he nodded his acceptance of them with wary eyes. "What about Ulrick and Mer—"

"Ulrick, my friend, to use an old mining term, has 'cratered.' Once he realized Hazel McCallum put the governor on his butt, he broke down and blubbered like a baby. Immediately made a deal with me to turn state's evidence in exchange for a strong recommendation for a reduced sentence. Even as we speak, he's in the protective custody of the Witness Protection Program. And I hear he's singing like a canary in paradise.''

Quinn, who had remained standing since he arrived, now had to sit down, and quick.

For the rest of her life Constance would remember the look in his eyes as his gaze touched hers—the look of a man who expected to die in surgery, but instead woke up healthy and healed.

''So he's even fingering Dolph Merriday?'' Quinn asked, still incredulous.

''Call the roll, buddy. Merriday, Jeremy Schrader, Brandon Whitaker—all the key players get a big, sloppy Judas kiss,'' Mumford confirmed. ''Not to brag, but ATF already even busted the hit men in the SUV, got them locked down on federal firearms charges.''

''Tell them to let their lab crew go over Connie's Jeep,'' Quinn interjected. ''Add attempted murder one, hit for hire, to those charges. They opened fire on us late last night.''

''Dolph doesn't know all this yet,'' Mumford resumed. ''Right now he's out at a political fund-raiser at Hathaway Country Club, glad-handing the next sucker who might vote for him. He's already got a press release ready, announcing his run for the state senate. Goodbye to all that.''

''Merriday will slug it out to the bitter end,'' Quinn pointed out. ''He's not as weak-kneed as Ulrick.''

''Let him fight,'' Mumford scoffed. ''These guys

figured they had the keys to the mint, Quinn, and then you come along. You two,'' he amended, looking at Constance. ''But now, with the governor's blessings, we're going to flush all these sleazebags down the toilet at once. Bring some new blood out here.''

''Even Judge Winston came on board?'' Quinn said skeptically. ''Lad, I fired shots in his courtroom. And that guy is a rule-book commando.''

''Yeah,'' Mumford admitted, ''that was touch-and-go, at first. But he's always liked you and despised Merriday—hinted as much, anyway, when I spoke to him. What decided him was when both U.S. marshals told him you deliberately aimed high. The bullet holes confirmed that—three feet over their heads. In light of the conspiracy, Winston decided your actions could be stretched to fit a self-defense claim.''

By now Constance couldn't keep the tears of joy and relief from brimming over her quivering eyelids. A huge weight had been lifted from her, and she felt almost as if she might float right up to the ceiling.

She even dared to hope that it had changed the essential impasse between her and Quinn. He was a man of honor; he'd been vindicated as she knew he would. And perhaps he'd see that he was good enough for her. Too good, perhaps. His struggle for justice had become hers, and together—with Hazel's eleventh-hour help—they had won.

''I better warn both of you,'' Mumford added. ''Get set for a media circus. A press release goes out today, timed for release just after Dolph and the rest are slapped with indictments and arrested. And by order of the governor, both of you figure prominently in the story—as citizen-heroes who stood up to corrupt thugs.''

Mumford smiled at Constance. "The little town of Mystery is going to be overwhelmed for the next few days. Hey, ask a favor? If you meet Barbara Walters, get her autograph for my wife, okay? It's Debb, with two *b*s. She'd kill me if I didn't ask."

The agent seemed to see the long look exchanged by his visitors, a look that clearly suggested they wished they could be alone to talk.

He stood up. "If you two'll excuse me, I've got stuff to run off in the copying room. Hold down the fort for a few minutes."

Discreetly, Todd pulled the office door shut as he left.

In the roller-coaster ride of emotions today, Constance had been able to postpone thoughts about this very moment—the time when Quinn would finally be safe. Safe, but not hers. The time when the terrifying adventure ended and they would be forced to sort out what was real and enduring, and what was simply the product of anxiety and fear.

Her heart was heavy, and she wasn't sure how long she could hold her feelings in check. She spoke first, staying in the chair because her legs were suddenly trembling.

"Quinn, I know we talked about…about us earlier—and I know you think nothing's changed between us. I guess I can see that in your eyes right now, but—"

He held up his hand, silencing her. "Everything has changed. And it's happened so quickly I can hardly take it in yet."

"Now you can go back to your old life, free and clear of all that's happened," she murmured, almost to herself. "You can go back to the U.S. Attorney's office again.'' She looked up at him. ''But when you do return to your old life, if you got nothing out of our—our—relationship, then please take this with you—*you* convinced me you were a man of honor. *You* convinced me in spite of your background, in spite of everything. I believed it before Agent Mumford did. So it's in you, Quinn. It *is* you. You needn't worry about your demons any longer. Because they lie.''

She looked away from him, the pain too intense. ''The governor is right. You *are* a hero. A swash-buckling swordsman, just like in real life.''

She didn't know if her words meant anything to him. But suddenly she felt his strong hands on her small shoulders. He bent down to her, his expression tight with constrained emotion.

''If you're going to dish out flattery, you'll have to take some, too,'' he told her in the rough voice she knew so well. ''I have never, in my entire life, known anyone as loyal as you, and I don't mean loyal like a good, simple dog. I mean loyal like a guardian an-gel—a beautiful, smart and gutsy angel.''

''Then I must be a fallen angel.'' She gave him a sad, rueful smile. ''What I felt in bed with you was pretty earthy,'' she admitted.

She almost lost her taut control. She'd stayed so strong through the past tumultuous days, but this last meeting—nothing could feel more precarious. It was sweet agony to her—one emotional trial too many. Hazel said he was a keeper. But there was no way to keep someone against his own self-divided will.

She forced herself to breathe deeply as she recalled something else Hazel told her: *Do what you believe is right, and risk the consequences.* That advice inspired her now as she faced down this man she loved with all her troubled heart.

"You amaze me, Quinn Loudon. Just look at the risks you've taken to see these creeps prosecuted. You put your life on the line."

She rose, and he stood with her. She raised her right hand to gently touch the bullet graze on his cheek.

"You put your life on the line for justice. But I wonder if you can do it for something else. Something bigger."

"And what would that be?" His face was stone hard, his expression inscrutable.

"Love."

"I could insult your intelligence and deny that," he confessed. "But I won't. You're right. But knowing the risk is worth it in your mind isn't the same as somehow reprogramming your heart."

She stared at him for a long terrible moment. It was clear he didn't feel what she felt. She had finally found a prince, but he wanted a princess, not a workaholic real estate agent from little old Mystery. The hurt swelled inside, but she shoved it down. She would have a lot of long nights to think about the past few days. She would have a lot of long nights to wallow in her wounds.

Smiling through glistening eyes, she said, "At one time I had all the reason in the world to be down on myself and men. Still, I…well, I guess I found out I'm a lot braver than I thought I was. I let down my guard but good. And I don't regret it, even as much as this—this—" With a supreme effort she forced down a sob. She didn't finish.

He put his arms around her. It was a fortress. One

she longed to remain in. For perhaps twenty seconds her tears dampened the front of his—Doug's—shirt.

But summoning an iron will she hadn't known she possessed, she stepped back from his embrace and quickly dried her eyes with a tissue from a box on Mumford's desk.

"Connie—"

This time it was her turn to put up her hand and silence him.

She choked back a grim laugh. "We've both had a couple of insane days. Should we make decisions that might affect the rest of our lives on three days of running from the law? That would be stupid."

"So we take our time. We think about it," he offered.

She glanced at him. He was giving her the Back-away Words. The "Can't We Just Be Friends," line.

But they would never be friends. She loved him. He'd brought out a passion within her that she didn't know existed. She would never be the same woman ever again.

Never.

She didn't want that to be the final word between them. But she knew that she was on the verge of losing control completely.

"I have to get back to Mystery. I've missed work. Everyone's looking for me. "

He said nothing. He just stared at her, frozen.

In that awful moment, she realized that heartache was not a metaphor—the hurt inside her chest felt like a stab wound. Barely restraining tears, she brushed his lips lightly with hers. Whispering, she mouthed the word, *Goodbye* in his ear. Then she escaped into the hallway.

* * *

Constance was so despondent that she felt numb. Emotionally Novacained, she quickly set out on the return drive to Mystery alone, still shattered by the prophetic word: *Never.*

She knew from experience, it took a long time to accept the word *Never.* "Possibly," was something that kept coming up in the human heart. *Possibly Doug was going to come back to her and tell her it was all a mistake. Possibly Doug was going to clear up her credit card problems and tell her the hotel rooms were for someone else, not his other lovers.*

The possiblys took a long time to work through. Years sometimes. A lifetime even.

But once she hit the brick wall of *never,* as broken and hurting as she would be, she knew she could finally accept it.

As she would have to force herself to accept it now.

She and Quinn were different people with different lives. They never would have even met if not for fate and circumstance—and it was a bad fate and bad circumstances that had driven them together.

It was not the beginning of a hopeful relationship.

Besides, she still knew very little about Quinn Loudon. She might know what was inside his heart and his soul, but the practical things were non-existent. She didn't even know if he was engaged or dating someone. For all she knew, he was ready to tie the knot when he got shot.

A relationship between them was absurd. They were strangers, really. They knew nothing useful about each other.

Except what was inside each other's heart and soul.

She steeled herself against the hopefulness.

Merging onto the interstate, she upbraided herself with brutal clarity of mind.

She and Quinn were just one of those things, and she'd just have to accept it. She would probably never see Quinn Loudon again, not even in court—her deposition was all they would need with a confession, not her appearance.

It was now over, and it had truly been nothing more than a fling fraught with danger—indeed, she admonished herself, maybe it was even the "danger sex" she craved most, some strange psychological compensation for her staid, "good girl" existence.

But it would never work between them.

Never, she told herself again and again, praying the hope would die with every beat of her heart.

Still emotionally propping herself up, Connie stopped, only one hour west of Billings. She was still out of clear cell phone range thanks to the mountains, so she had to use a pay phone at a truck plaza. Dutifully she placed three calls, to her mother, Hazel, and Ginny, assuring all of them she was fine and on her way home.

She offered no details, promising more to come, but her duty done, the inevitable happened. Only five minutes after she returned to the swirling snow haze of the interstate, hot tears abruptly began spilling from her eyes.

She needed a good cry, but she knew this wasn't the best weather for tear-blurred vision. Still, the sadness that welled up inside her each time she recalled the grim finality of their parting only forced more teardrops to roll down her cheeks.

As if life hadn't dumped on her enough lately, a flashing blue gumball appeared in the rearview mirror and dogged her.

It's the crunched-up rear end of the Jeep, she guessed, hurriedly trying to wipe her eyes. Probably a brakelight was out. Now she would get a ticket in addition to everything else.

Depressed and resigned, she flipped on the right-turn signal and slowed, pulling off as wide as she could on the snow-clogged shoulder of the highway. A big rig whooshed by, rocking the Jeep. She parked and rolled down her window, waiting for the trooper.

A form, indiscernible in the blowing whiteness, stepped out of the passenger's side of the cruiser.

A second later she almost cried out when her own passenger's door flew open.

Before she could even recover from her fright, Quinn was sitting beside her. He cupped her face with warm hands.

"After you left," he told her, "I asked Todd to leave me alone some more. I did nothing but think about us. You know what? I think you *did* reprogram my heart. All I know is, I don't want to be without you."

Not sure if his words were still welcome to her ears, he added in a more joking tone, "Think there are any jobs in Mystery suitable for an Assistant U.S. Attorney?"

She couldn't speak. It seemed like a dream. His coming out of the whiteout seemed like she had somehow conjured him from the cold storm of her hope. She touched his face to be sure that it was real. He was. Warm and strong. The man she remembered. The man she knew.

A tumult of emotions closed her throat. She let the ardor of a kiss answer for her, even as she realized: she was still a little afraid that the adventure of true love might be even more harrowing than the one she'd just experienced.

But she was determined to go along for the ride. As she had the last one. On belief alone.

As for a job suitable for Quinn—in her mind she could already hear Hazel declaring they'd *make* a job for him if one didn't exist. The Matriarch of Mystery had already made it clear that Quinn rated aces high with her. And Constance knew part of the old girl's motivation was quite personal—the secret glee of a successful matchmaker.

When he pulled back to study her face, she was startled by the intense seriousness of those smoke-tinted eyes.

"I have to ask this right now," he told her, "and no matter what, I want the truth. Promise?"

She nodded, her heart racing with fearful suspense.

"Can you really love me after all I put you through? Not just now in the flush of emotions. I mean—later, when all this sinks in?"

"I can, I do, and I will," she assured him without a moment's hesitation. "After your initial deception to lure me into the cabin, when you were bleeding and desperate, you were always right up front with me. Every single detail you told me turned out to be true."

She paused and flashed him a rueful smile through tears that were now welcome—tears of joy.

"What?" he demanded.

"It's just awfully ironic," she explained as their

lips drew ineluctably closer and closer together, "that the first honest man I ever found—" their lips met...and both felt the current of pleasure "—kidnapped me," she finished breathlessly.

Epilogue

Hazel McCallum looked down at the telegram in her hand. It was from Paris. A sly smile tipped the corner of her lips as she moved them to read it in silence.

Dear Hazel,
Quinn and I were married today here. We wished you were here but we had to leave quickly to get away from the publicity. I never knew the press would be so excited about our romance on the run! We are thinking of you. You were our matron of honor in spirit. We'll see you as soon as we return to Mystery. Quinn is excited about our new log home by the river. He told me today to name our baby Hazel—but what if it's a boy? Jake, then?

With love,
Connie and Quinn

As she was now in the habit of doing, Hazel went to Jake McCallum's portrait and put another notch in the walnut frame. Number two match was made. Jacquelyn and A.J. were first. Third was coming up.

She mused on all the possibilities. There were so many fine folks in Mystery who needed pairing up. But it wasn't always the obvious ones. Sometimes they just appeared on the doorstep, needing her help or sometimes they—

The phone rang, interrupting her thoughts.

She picked it up and said automatically in her no-nonsense voice, "McCallum Ranch."

"Hazel?"

"As right as rain."

The laugh was familiar at the other end. "And don't I know it. I'm your doctor, remember?"

Hazel narrowed her eyes. "Doctor? Is that what you call yourself?" She gave a hrrumph. "A doctor goes out in a snowstorm and births babies. A doctor dispenses wisdom with his prescriptions. When was the last time you did that, you wet-behind-the-ears geriatric specialist?"

"Give me some time, Hazel, and I promise to do all that and more. Just give me some time."

"Time? You're in your thirties and you haven't even started a family. You're running out of time, if I set my watch correctly—"

Hazel looked at the phone in amazement.

She didn't even hear Dr. Saville mumble, "Maybe I could get to that if all my patients weren't so difficult. Now are you taking the blood pressure medicine I prescribed or do I have to come out there for myself to see you take it..."

A big gorgeous smile creased her face.

Sometimes the needy folk just appeared on the doorstep, and then sometimes they called you up on the phone to annoy you about your medications.

She took a look at Jake McCallum's portrait with the two notches on the frame. She smiled and thought: *Yep, I think I'll put the next notch right over there.*

* * * * *

*Don't miss the next book
in Meagan McKinney's*

MATCHED IN MONTANA series!

*Look for Dr. John Saville's story,
THE M.D. COURTS HIS NURSE,
coming in March 2001 from Silhouette Desire.*

"Who writes the best romance fiction today?
No doubt it's Jayne Ann Krentz."
—*Affaire de Coeur*

JAYNE ANN KRENTZ

writes compelling stories that
keep her fans demanding more!

Be sure to look for these
other stories originally written as

STEPHANIE JAMES

NIGHTWALKER
FABULOUS BEAST
NIGHT OF THE MAGICIAN
THE SILVER SNARE
THE DEVIL TO PAY
TO TAME THE HUNTER

*Available this October wherever
Silhouette Books are sold.*

#1 *New York Times* bestselling author

NORA ROBERTS

introduces the loyal and loving, tempestuous and tantalizing Stanislaski family.

Coming in November 2000:

The Stanislaski Brothers

Mikhail and Alex

Their immigrant roots and warm, supportive home had made Mikhail and Alex Stanislaski both strong and passionate. And their charm makes them irresistible....

In February 2001, watch for
THE STANISLASKI SISTERS: Natasha and Rachel

And a brand-new Stanislaski story from Silhouette Special Edition,
CONSIDERING KATE

Available at your favorite retail outlet.

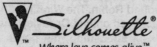

♥ Silhouette® —
where love comes alive—online...

eHARLEQUIN.com

shop eHarlequin

♥ Find all the new Silhouette releases at everyday great discounts.

♥ Try before you buy! Read an excerpt from the latest Silhouette novels.

♥ Write an online review and share your thoughts with others.

reading room

♥ Read our Internet exclusive daily and weekly online serials, or vote in our interactive novel.

♥ Talk to other readers about your favorite novels in our Reading Groups.

♥ Take our Choose-a-Book quiz to find the series that matches you!

authors' alcove

♥ Find out interesting tidbits and details about your favorite authors' lives, interests and writing habits.

♥ Ever dreamed of being an author? Enter our Writing Round Robin. The Winning Chapter will be published online! Or review our writing guidelines for submitting your novel.

You're not going to believe this offer!

In October and November 2000, buy any two Harlequin or Silhouette books and save $10.00 off future purchases, or buy any three and save $20.00 off future purchases!

Just fill out this form and attach 2 proofs of purchase (cash register receipts) from October and November 2000 books and Harlequin will send you a coupon booklet worth a total savings of $10.00 off future purchases of Harlequin and Silhouette books in 2001. Send us 3 proofs of purchase and we will send you a coupon booklet worth a total savings of $20.00 off future purchases.

Saving money has never been this easy.

I accept your offer! Please send me a coupon booklet:

Name: _____

Address: _____ City: _____

State/Prov.: _____ Zip/Postal Code: _____

Optional Survey!

In a typical month, how many Harlequin or Silhouette books would you buy <u>new</u> at retail stores?

☐ Less than 1   ☐ 1   ☐ 2   ☐ 3 to 4   ☐ 5+

Which of the following statements best describes how you <u>buy</u> Harlequin or Silhouette books? Choose one answer only that <u>best</u> describes you.

☐ I am a regular buyer and reader
☐ I am a regular reader but buy only occasionally
☐ I only buy and read for specific times of the year, e.g. vacations
☐ I subscribe through Reader Service but also buy at retail stores
☐ I mainly borrow and buy only occasionally
☐ I am an occasional buyer and reader

Which of the following statements best describes how you <u>choose</u> the Harlequin and Silhouette series books you buy <u>new</u> at retail stores? By "series," we mean books within a particular line, such as *Harlequin PRESENTS* or *Silhouette SPECIAL EDITION*. Choose one answer only that <u>best</u> describes you.

☐ I only buy books from my favorite series
☐ I generally buy books from my favorite series but also buy books from other series on occasion
☐ I buy some books from my favorite series but also buy from many other series regularly
☐ I buy all types of books depending on my mood and what I find interesting and have no favorite series

---

Please send this form, along with your cash register receipts as proofs of purchase, to:
In the U.S.: Harlequin Books, P.O. Box 9057, Buffalo, NY 14269
In Canada: Harlequin Books, P.O. Box 622, Fort Erie, Ontario L2A 5X3

(Allow 4-6 weeks for delivery) Offer expires December 31, 2000.   PHQ4002

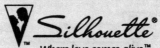

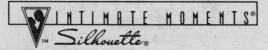

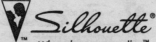

INTIMATE MOMENTS®

TM Silhouette®

COMING NEXT MONTH

**#1039 THE BRANDS WHO CAME FOR CHRISTMAS—
Maggie Shayne**

The Oklahoma All-Girl Brands

After one incredible night spent in the arms of a stranger, Maya Brand
found herself pregnant—with twins! But when her mystery man
reappeared and claimed he wanted to be part of their lives, was Maya
ready to trust Caleb Montgomery with her expected bundles of joy—
and with her own fragile heart?

#1040 HERO AT LARGE—Robyn Amos

A Year of Loving Dangerously

SPEAR agent Keshon Gray was on a mission that could ultimately get
him killed. So when his one and only love, Rennie Williams, re-entered
his life, Keshon wasn't about to let her get too close. But knowing she
was near forced Keshon to re-evaluate his life. If he survived his mission,
would he consider starting over with the woman he couldn't resist?

#1041 MADE FOR EACH OTHER—Doreen Owens Malek

FBI bodyguard Tony Barringer knew he shouldn't mix business with
pleasure when it came to protecting Jill Darcy and her father from a
series of threats. After all, Tony was around for very different reasons—
ones Jill *definitely* wouldn't be happy about. So until he got his answers,
Tony had to hold out—no matter what his heart demanded.

#1042 HERO FOR HIRE—Marie Ferrarella

ChildFinders, Inc.

Detective Chad Andreini was more than willing to help beautiful
Veronica Lancaster find her kidnapped son—*but* she insisted on helping
with the investigation. So they teamed up, determined to bring the boy
back home. But once the ordeal was over, could this unlikely pair put
their own fears aside and allow their passions to take over?

#1043 DANGEROUS LIAISONS—Maggie Price

Nicole Taylor's business was love matches, not murder. Until her dating-
service clients started turning up dead. Suddenly she found herself
suspected, then safeguarded, by Sergeant Jake Ford. And falling hard for
the brooding top cop who no longer believed in love.

#1044 DAD IN BLUE—Shelley Cooper

Samantha Underwood would do whatever it took to help her eight-year-
old son recover from the loss of his father. And thanks to sexy police
chief Carlo Garibaldi, the boy seemed to be improving. But when it came
to love, Carlo was a tough man to convince—until Samantha showed him
just how good it could be....